April

LIE LIKE A WOMAN

OTHER NOVELS by April Campbell Jones:

Die Like a Man: a Bree and Richard Matthews Mystery

BRACKEN AND BLEDSOE PARANORMAL MYSTERIES:

Fever Dreams

Night Chills

Dark Visions

VAMPIRE POODLE SERIES:

Mitzi Magee: Vampire Poodle

Mitzi Magee: Blood Scent

Mitzi Magee: A Nip in Time

LIE LIKE A WOMAN

LIE LIKE A WOMAN

April Campbell Jones

rover press

LIE LIKE A WOMAN

A Rover Press Book

DEDICATION:

*To my soulmate and
to my children,
without whom there'd be nothing
to write about...*

LIE LIKE A WOMAN

CHAPTER ONE

I looked over at the clock. It was 5:00 a.m.

"You awake?"

"Naturally."

"Thinking about a plot?"

"Not exactly..."

There was a silence then and I could visualize her lying there in the darkness, biting her lip. Bree always bites her lower lip when she's trying to make a decision. Somehow this makes her sexier than she already is, which is considerably sexy to begin with, and visualizing her doing this made me visualize her doing other things.

"Richard?"

"What?"

"Charlie called today..."

My visualizations vanished and I turned my back to her and pretended to snore. Of course this did absolutely no good. She sat up abruptly in bed beside me and shook my shoulder, her excitement palpable.

"Richard, listen to me! Charlie says they've uncovered something really important--"

"I don't want to hear about it."

"You know that house they're reconstructing on Adams? Just up the block?"

"What about it?"

"Charlie says when they tore down the west wall today, they found a skeleton!"

"Good night, Bree..."

"Oh, come on, Richard, I want to go *see*."

Her green eyes were shining there in the dark and I had to smile. She was such a fine-boned, delicate creature, a nymph from some bygone era; no one would ever dream, looking at her, that she was so bloodthirsty. But then, I should have known. Our first date had taken place in a police morgue.

"Why can't you make things up out of your head like other writers?"

"I'm not talented enough...Richard? Don't play 'possum! I know you don't have anything scheduled for tomorrow, I checked with Rita."

I made a mental note to fire Rita.

"Go by yourself. Or have Charlie take you. You don't need me."

She snuggled up against my back, her small hands curling around my chest. Of course she knew she was irresistible, and my resistance factor was never very high anyway.

"I don't know why I have to come," I growled, without much conviction.

"Someone has to look out for the baby..." she cooed.

* * *

Ever since we've had Margaret, Bree has insisted on taking her everywhere. When Margaret was a small baby this didn't present a particular problem; Bree just carried her papoose-style in a backpack. Sometimes she got funny looks, but that's only because you don't see too many babies at the scenes of savage crimes. But now that Margaret was a rambunctious two-year-old it was becoming more and more absurd. True, she's as cute as a button and could charm a rattlesnake, not a bad trait to have in a town as full of rattlesnakes as this one, but lately I've noticed that my contacts are more reluctant to give me information and the Chief of Police seems to wince every time he sees me coming. I tell Bree it's about time we hired some help; she ignores me.

So promptly at eight the next morning I'm bundling Margaret into her car seat, along with all her paraphernalia: diaper bag, animal crackers, extra rompers in case there's an accident (inevitable), three stuffed bears and a sexy silk nightgown I bought Bree for that trip to Catalina we never took. Margaret has taken to carrying the nightgown everywhere, referring to it as her "silky". I've tried weaning her away from it but it does no good. She's as tenaciously attached to it as Linus is to his blanket.

I honk the horn and Bree comes running out of the house, breathless. She is wide awake as usual; she never seems to sleep. Her hair, which I finally persuaded her to grow out last year, flounces in a smooth auburn rush around her shoulders, and she's wearing her glasses, which always means serious business. I sigh. What is it about this ridiculous woman I find so appealing? Admittedly I'm not the only one--I have never met anyone, man or woman, who isn't crazy about Bree.

She smiles radiantly at me. "Ready?"

I shrug. She reaches over and squeezes my earlobe, one of her little gestures. I always wonder when she does that whether she used to do the same thing to Charlie. Charlie is Bree's ex-husband, and my nemesis. Charlie doesn't realize that he's my nemesis; after all, they were already divorced when I met Bree. As a matter of fact, if anyone asked him, Charlie would say that he's my best friend. And he was, too, before I knew Bree. We worked together a lot in the days when he first joined the force and I was the new boy at my dad's agency. I used to think he was a pretty good cop, and after work there was this bar, the High Time, where we used to spend the hours cruising the talent. That was quite a while ago, of course, when everyone did that, and everybody was sleeping with everybody else. And Charlie *always* scored, even though he was balding and twenty pounds overweight. He looked like a guy. A *real* guy. Girls thought he was masculine yet harmless, and that was Charlie's strong suit. Easy going, appealing in a puppy-dog way. I scared the girls off with my intensity. All the time we were going to the High Time, I never scored. Not once. But Charlie--Charlie never went home alone.

When I pulled the Mustang up beside the house on Adams, Charlie was the first person I saw. He grinned and waved. Like Bree, he seemed tireless and forever cheerful, and for a short, uncontrolled moment, I hated his guts. Bree jumped out of the car, ran to him, and kissed his cheek. I went around to her side and reached for Margaret.

"Daddy?" she asked tentatively. "That's me," I answered grimly, twisting my back as I pulled her out of the car seat. I set her down on her sturdy little legs and attempted to fasten her leash to her wrist. It was like trying to wrestle an alligator. Finally I gave up and grabbed her hand. "Hold on," I warned her sternly. We walked over to Bree and Charlie. Charlie let out a whoop and threw Margaret up into the sky. "How's my little Maggie?" he shouted. Margaret dissolved in a cascade of giggles. She adores Charlie.

"Hiya, Rick!" I nodded. Charlie put Margaret down and she immediately escaped, darting past several plainclothesmen who were trying to dust the remaining ravaged wall for prints. It was typical of local police procedure that they would waste their time doing this. I could have told them that it was pointless.

"Neat, huh? Don't find very many skeletons bricked into walls these days."

"Have you identified it yet?"

"Nope. Looks female, but the pelvis is crushed so it's hard to say. Wanna play racketball later?"

"Can't," I lied, "I've got a hot date."

Bree ignored me. She's impossible to offend anyway; I've practically given up trying. Charlie guffawed. For some reason he's always found me funny. Or maybe he was just laughing *at* me, remembering my lack of success with the opposite sex.

Bree tugged at Charlie. "Who owns this house?"

Charlie checked his notes. "Carl Bakersfield. Bought it three years ago. Lives here with someone named Perry Sinker. No relation."

"Gay?"

"I assume. They haven't denied it. They're staying at Bakersfield's mansion in La Jolla while the house is being renovated. Bakersfield apparently inherited money and played the market with it. Doubled it in a year. Perry I don't know about yet. I'm checking."

Bree suddenly decided it was time to leave. "Margaret!" she yelled. All the plainclothesmen turned toward her, surprised to hear such a loud sound come out of such a small person. Margaret peeked around a corner, her impish face split in a grin. She launched herself into Bree's arms.

"See you later, Charlie. Richard's got to get to work."

"Lunch on Thursday as usual?"

"Sure," she said absently, staring at the broken wall, "I'll call you." We got into the car. I had to squeeze into the passenger side, nearly crushing the family jewels in the process. Bree leaves the seat up practically to the dash. I threw it back and accidentally jammed it against Margaret's car seat. "Daddy! Hurt feet!" Margaret screamed. I pushed it forward a little and Bree pulled the car away from the curb. Since we only have one car she was going to have to drop me off at the office, an incredible inconvenience for me but just another example of Bree's quirks. To her more than one car to a family was an extravagant excess, and Bree *hates* excess.

I cleared my throat. "Am I mistaken, or did I hear you make a date with your ex-husband back there?"

Bree drove along silently for a second. Then: "Why do you think someone would have plastered a body in a wall with a ravine nearby? It would have been so much simpler just to bury it..."

"Coyotes, remember? The ravine is full of them, they would have dug it up in a second."

Bree frowned. "Maybe it's an old body. Maybe there were no coyotes in the ravine when the body was killed."

"Bodies aren't killed. People are killed and become bodies." I sighed. "Are you seeing Charlie on the sly?"

Bree suddenly realized what I was saying and looked at me in shock. "That isn't a serious question."

I stuck out my lip. "It is too."

She smiled slightly. "Well, it isn't exactly on the sly..."

"What does that mean?"

"That means that Charlie and I have lunch occasionally so I can pump him for interesting gruesome details for the sake of art, and I always take a chaperone." She gestured toward the back seat. "He only sees me because he's in love with Margaret."

"I'm not so sure..." I said darkly. I was feeling particularly grouchy this morning and I wasn't quite ready to let this drop. "If this is on the up-and-up, why didn't you tell me about it before?"

"There's nothing to tell," she answered lightly, pulling the car up in front of the downtown Wells Fargo Bank Building. "Now go to work."

I leaned over to kiss her and she reluctantly presented her cheek. She hates public shows of affection between adults, although she doesn't think anything of bussing Margaret's fat tummy in the middle of a crowded restaurant. I felt cheated. It was obvious I was insecure and in need of reassurance, and all she could think about was the damned skeleton in the wall.

"Get Pop to bring you home, okay? I've got things to do."

She had that distant look in her eye again and I knew we were off and running. It had been too long between books for her and she was chaffing at the bit. I stepped back from the car and she roared off into the traffic. I was confident I wouldn't see her again for a long time...

CHAPTER TWO

"You're late again," said Rita, the traitorous bitch, as I walked through the glass door. I was particularly proud of that glass door. Just this year the painter had come out to alter the sign from **The Matthews Agency** to **Matthews and Matthews** and it always gave me a little thrill, seeing that as I walked in. Naturally Rita ruined it for me. She had a way of throwing a soggy towel in my face whenever she thought I looked too happy.

"Here are your messages," she said, handing me a pile of yellow slips. I remembered that I had planned to fire her this morning and glared at her angrily, trying to look as threatening as possible. She smiled back, her perfect white teeth glistening against perfect red lips set against impossibly perfect porcelain skin framed by perfect black silky hair. Dad had hired her last year in a fit of lust, and admittedly she was the most stunning female I'd ever seen off a movie screen. She was tall and lushly built and she moved like a bored panther, and Dad was on the verge of a perpetual heart attack just having her here.

Unfortunately, she was also the smartest, most competent secretary I'd ever had, and even though we couldn't stand each other, I had to admit the business would probably go bankrupt without her. My threatening look wilted and I busied myself with my messages.

The first one was from Dolores Zapata, whose estranged husband had stolen their thirteen-year-old twin boys three months earlier.

"It's ain't that I want them back," she had explained when she'd hired me to track them down, "It's just that I want to personally cut the balls off that son-of-a-bitch for not taking them earlier, if he's still alive. They've probably tortured him to death and disposed of the remains by now, if I know my boys!" Their names were Donnie and Lonnie, and from the picture of them their mother gave me, I thought it perfectly possible that they had dispatched their father by now. I was having no luck tracing him, at any rate. I decided not to call Dolores back until tomorrow.

The second message was from Bree's mother, who had called me long distance to tell me that she and Bree's father were flying in from Kansas City next week for Bree's birthday, and it was to be kept secret from Bree until I brought them home from the airport. Bree's mother, Helen, had hinted at this plan last month but I'd tried to ignore it; now it looked like I was going to be stuck in the middle again. Knowing Bree, it was not going to be exactly the kind of surprise that would have her turning cartwheels on her birthday. In fact, she was liable to divorce me for my part in it, or at least split my head open with a red hot poker.

It wasn't that Bree didn't love her parents, and want to see them as often as possible. But because Bree is a writer, most people assume she has nothing to do all day long except entertain them. It was impossible for them to understand that Bree works constantly, even when she's just standing there. The thinking is the hard part of writing, especially the kind of writing Bree does, and right now Bree was trying to give birth to a new plot. For her it was as painful as giving birth to a baby. It was for me, too. I hate this part. I always end up feeling left out of her life. Her most recent book was published this month, but she'd completed it last spring, and for two months she'd been an absolute delight, charming, outgoing, enticing; it had been like a second honeymoon. Then about a month ago she began to withdraw, to walk the floors at night, and I knew what was coming. I'd been through it three times since we got married. The first time had been a shock; I thought she'd been seeing another man and I was sure I would lose her. In a way, I was right. She had been seeing Joshua Mood. He was really her first love. She had known him long before she knew me, and in a way I couldn't blame her for loving him more. He was, after all, a far better man than I, and a far more efficient detective. And although he was a confirmed bachelor, I'm convinced that Bree would have married him in a second.

If he'd existed anyplace but in her mind. And in the minds of her readers.

The Joshua Mood detective series was a big success for Bree; her first, really. Before Joshua she'd written a couple of esoteric, difficult mainstream novels that nobody read, and then she'd given up writing for a few years while she was married to Charlie. But somewhere in the back of her brain Joshua was percolating even then, just waiting for a chance to appear. I'm convinced that's why she married Charlie. I'm sure she figured a working knowledge of police procedure might come in handy.

I also wondered whether she might have married *me* for the same reason. When Bree and I met, I had just started working at my dad's agency and she'd just published *Mood Swing*, the first Joshua Mood novel, to rave reviews. Our first five dates were interrupted by police calls. In those days Bree kept a squawk box in her Jeep, and she insisted on picking me up, just in case she should miss anything. She is fanatical about detail. By the time she realized I didn't fit into the hard-boiled detective mold, we already gotten married.

"Ahem!" Rita poked me hard in the ribs. Subtlety was never one of her strong points. I jerked back to reality. These days I was always daydreaming. I looked at the third message.

From Charlie, naturally. Apparently Margaret had lifted a piece of evidence from the scene of the crime and did I know where Bree was today?

I tossed the messages into the wastebasket. Rita frowned. "I know there was something I wanted to tell you, but I can't remember what just now."

I stood there patiently.

"Oh, yes! Your father wants you."

I sighed and headed to my father's office. His door said: **Richard Matthews, Sr.** I started to turn the knob. "He's got a client in there," Rita warned. I decided to knock instead.

"Come on in, Rick. Meet Mr. Bakersfield."

I walked into the office. In the large leather chair reserved for clients sat a tall, handsome man with sandy hair and freckles. He was wearing a beautifully tailored business suit, and the freckles in no way distracted from the dignity and seriousness of his features. He looked like visiting royalty. I stuck out my hand.

"How do you do?"

He pressed it with just the right amount of firmness. "My pleasure."

I turned to Dad, looking for a clue. Dad was obviously overcome with the possibilities of the situation. I'll say one thing for my Dad: he's always been able to smell money a mile away, and right now it was all he could do to keep from sniffing the air like a bloodhound. Mr. Bakersfield exuded the scent of dollars, old dollars. It was an aroma that always conjured the deepest respect in my father.

"Ah, Mr. Bakersfield has come to us with a delicate matter, a *very* delicate matter." His tone was hushed, grave.

Bakersfield turned to me. "Yes, Mr. Matthews, I'm afraid I have."

I sat down on the hardback chair opposite him. It was Dad's theory that his agents should always be uncomfortable. He felt this contributed to alertness. Consequently I always ended the day with a sore ass.

"What seems to be the problem, Mr. Bakersfield?"

The man's face turned sorrowful and his eyes seemed slightly wetter. "Infidelity, Mr. Matthews. It's a horrible thing. Have you ever suspected a loved one of infidelity?"

I remembered Bree's lunch date with Charlie.

"I suspect my dear one of being unfaithful, Mr. Matthews, and I wish to hire your agency to confirm that suspicion. I don't want to make accusations without proof." He turned his head away. It was obviously very difficult for a man in his position to admit these things to strangers, and I felt sorry for him. Still, it was another five or ten thousand in the coffers, and things had been a little slow this fall. Couldn't hurt.

I looked at Dad. Any show of honest emotion always impresses him. I could tell he was in awe of this guy.

"Well, that's what we're here for, Mr. Bakersfield. We'll start today. It would help if we had a picture--"

"I brought one. I thought it might be useful."

He reached into a leather briefcase on the floor beside him and brought out a color eight-by-ten portrait, shoving it at me, his face pale. "There's my darling."

I stared at it for a minute. It was a picture of a striking young man with deep blue eyes and a dimple in each cheek, sitting lazily on the deck of a yacht. There was something in those deep blue eyes that made me think Mr. Bakersfield was probably right about his suspicions. I handed the picture to Dad.

He choked. "But--but this is a *guy*!" he sputtered. I turned and gave him a sharp look. He shut up immediately. We both looked sympathetically at Mr. Bakersfield, who didn't seem to notice Dad's confusion.

"That's my Perry," he continued. "Beautiful, isn't he? We've been together for five years now, both of us ecstatically happy. I just can't understand..."

"Ah...Mr. Bakersfield, what makes you think that Perry is being--unfaithful?" Dad looked at me, exasperated. I shrugged. What difference did it make who was being unfaithful to whom? We needed the money.

Again Bakersfield seemed oblivious. "He's so *remote*, Mr. Matthews. You don't know Perry. He's always been open with me. Now I feel he's keeping secrets. He disappears for hours at a time, and when I ask him where he's been, he says he's been walking around shopping centers. Can you imagine? Shopping centers!"

He spat this last out as if the whole concept of shopping centers was obscene. This was a man who never set foot in a Sears-and-Roebuck in his life.

"Are you sure, Mr. Bakersfield, that you really want to know? Many of our clients wish they had never come to us."

His eyes darkened. "I must know. I must know."

Dad was speechless. Any passion not directly dealing to curvy female legs eluded him. I comforted Mr. Bakersfield as best I could, since I could see I wasn't going to get much help from the senior member of the firm.

"We'll need Perry's full name and age and his place of employment..."

"Perry Roland Sinker. He's twenty-seven. He's employed as my personal secretary."

"Perry Sinker? And you're Carl Bakersfield?"

He frowned at me suspiciously. "Yes?"

"But they found a skeleton in your house yesterday, didn't they?" I blurted out.

"That's right. How did you know that?" Bakersfield asked defensively. Now Dad was shooting daggers in my direction. He knew as well as I did, prejudices aside, that the firm needed this job, but my curiosity was piqued.

"I have a friend on the police force," I added casually.

Bakersfield relaxed, waving the question away as if he had nothing whatsoever to do with him. "That's nothing to be concerned about. A minor inconvenience. I've only owned the house for a few years; I've never lived there."

"Excuse me? I understood that you and Perry Sinker lived there together."

Bakersfield had a patient look that he no doubt reserved for incompetent underlings. "I bought the house for Perry as a birthday gift to do with it as he wished. After he moved into my house, he rented the bungalow out. Then last month he decided to renovate it. *Compres pas*? At any rate, that's not your concern. I'm interested in how Perry spends his afternoons, not how he spends his money. And I'm certain the local *gendarmes* have this skeleton affair well under control."

I was less certain but I decided to let the matter rest. We agreed on a price and Mr. Bakersfield left, assured that we would put a very discreet tail on his beloved Perry by tomorrow afternoon.

I asked Rita to run up a file on Perry Sinker. She's a whiz with the computer and she had it for me in less than a minute. Apparently this Perry guy had had a few casual run-ins with the law in his younger days, before he became a love god, and the local *gendarmes* were aware of it. I wondered if Bakersfield was aware of it. There was nothing major here, a couple of suspected drug deals, a drunk-and-disorderly, mostly minor infractions. And only one conviction, with a six-month jail term.

I handed the eight-by-ten to Rita and she looked at it curiously. "Missing person?"

"Infidelity."

She smiled enigmatically. "Ah. That explains it."

"What?"

"Why Mr. Bakersfield walked past my desk without pausing..."

On anyone else that would have sounded like undisguised egotism, but Rita was just being her usual blunt self. And of course she was right. No red-blooded heterosexual man could ever get past her without staring. Still, it annoyed me that she *knew* it. Everything about her annoyed me. I decided to start looking around discreetly for another secretary.

"Call Felton. See if he's busy. I need him to tail someone for me this week."

She indicated Perry's photo. "Loverboy?"

"Just call him."

"You bet, boss."

* * *

I had known Felton Shapiro since my college days. Even then he had looked middle-aged. He'd been working a security guard at the campus library. Otherwise I never would have noticed him. He is the most nondescript person I've ever met, about five-foot-five, with a slight potbelly and glasses, and a mousy balding pate, and even now I couldn't tell you what color his eyes are. He'd looked ridiculous in that security guard uniform, and eventually he'd gotten fired, not because he hadn't been good at his job, but because he'd looked ridiculous in his uniform. Actually he was very good at his job. He had an eagle eye and terrific instincts and could handle himself in a fight better than anyone. But the security department had been convinced that no perpetrator who got a look at that potbelly would take him seriously, and they'd let him go. By that time, we had gotten to know each other fairly well and we'd kept in touch. I used to spend a lot of time in the library in those days. That was when I was convinced that I was going to be the greatest lawyer this side of F. Lee Bailey. For a security guard Felton was extremely well read, and he'd always comment on whatever book I happened to be checking out that day. No matter what it was, he'd read it and had an opinion about it.

"*Ben Hur*? Too long. Not enough sex."

"*To Kill a Mockingbird*? Nice courtroom scene. Not enough sex."

No book ever qualified on the sex scale for Felton, but his opinions were not unconsidered. And I'd never found a book, fiction or non-fiction that Felton hadn't read.

After I'd dropped out of school in my senior year I'd looked Felton up. He had been turned away from the San Diego police department because he was too short and had opened up his own private detective agency on the East Side in a sleazy dive that can only be described as unappetizing. Unfortunately no one would hire him. He looked too much like an accountant.

At the time, I was still casting about trying to figure out what to do with my aborted law career, but my father was always looking for freelance agents and I'd decided to put in a good word for Felton. My father had never listened to me before on any matter of importance, but for some reason this time he'd taken my word for it and had decided to use Felton on a case. Felton had distinguished himself as I'd known he would and after that Dad had eyed me with a new respect. It wasn't long before he'd offered me a place with the firm, and the rest is history.

Now we used Felton whenever we could. He was the ideal tail. He blended into the woodwork perfectly because he as impossible to distinguish from the next guy, no matter who the next guy was. He was absolutely reliable, being neither susceptible to drink or women (or *men*, for that matter). Rita hated him. That endeared him to me all the more.

I decided to meet Felton after work at the Lonely Hunter, a steak-and-ale restaurant a block from the office. I tried to call Bree and let her know that I wouldn't be home for supper, but all I could raise was her voice on the answering machine: "*This is Bree Matthews. Neither Richard nor I are home, but if you'll leave your name and number, we'll get back to you...*" Getting the answering machine was no guarantee Bree wasn't home; she turned it on sometimes when she was working, or thinking, or when the baby was having a nap, but usually when she heard my voice she'd picked up the receiver. Tonight, nothing. It was already past six and I began to worry. I hate it when she runs around after dark by herself. Especially now that she takes the baby with her. I know that makes me sound like a chauvinist pig, and I guess I am. Women just seem more vulnerable. I didn't say they *were* more vulnerable, I just said they *seemed* that way. And if they seem that way to me, they're going to seem that way to the local mugger-rapist-slasher. I've told Bree a hundred times that she should carry a gun if she's going to parade around, but she says she'd rather die than kill someone else, and since this statement is in perfect keeping with Bree-philosophy there's really nothing I can say. Even throwing Margaret up to her does no good. As far as she's concerned, she's less vulnerable with the baby because everybody loves babies. Really brilliant reasoning.

Besides, it's all part of her work. Just like it's part of mine. Right?

* * *

Felton was sitting in the restaurant when I got there, thumbing through *The Reader*, San Diego's free press bonanza. He had the personal section open and as I approach him he said, "Get this, Richard. `*Forty year old black female with Mohawk wishes to meet shy tall stranger for tender encounters. Must love oysters, be proficient with cuffs and be willing to relocate.*'"

"I dunno about the tall part," he said uncertainly. "You think I could qualify on the basis of my personality?"

"Why not? *I'd* take you out."

Felton grinned. "Gee, thanks!" he said sincerely. His sense of the absurd was rather underdeveloped but his taste for kinkiness wasn't; I'd seen him with girls I wouldn't have touched with rubber gloves, several of whom looked as if they spent all their spare time in biker bars. I could never figure out how a guy like Felton landed all these Amazons.

"It never hurts to advertise..." said Felton cryptically. He put down the paper and we got to the matter at hand. I gave him Perry Sinker's picture and some background on the job. I didn't mention the skeleton.

"Sounds like a lead pipe cinch," said Felton. "By the way, I read Bree's new book last night..." he mentioned casually, "...you know--*Mood Over Miami...*"

"That's nice." I growled. Felton noticed my face and shut up abruptly. The waitress approached. She was maybe eighteen and stacked. I saw his eyes light up.

"What'll it be, fellas?"

Felton grinned. "How are your oysters?"

* * *

After dinner Felton gave me a lift home. He drives this paint-flaking rattletrap that's as nondescript as he is. Its heater hasn't worked for as long as I've known him and for some reason it was freezing outside. It's rare that the temperature in San Diego dips below sixty at night, but tonight it was all I could do to keep my teeth from chattering.

"Roll up the window, for God's sake!"

"Can't. Handle's broken." Felton chewed on a toothpick nonchalantly. "It's good, ya know. Just the right amount of sex..."

"What?"

"Bree's book."

I gritted my teeth. "There's the house, Felton. Don't go past it."

He pulled up to the curb and I struggled with the door. I never could understand why he didn't get a new car. With what we paid him and other jobs from the competing agencies in town, I knew he out-earned me.

"You gotta *kick* it," he offered, reaching one stubby leg across the seat and jamming it against the door hard. The door sprung open, nearly throwing me onto the sidewalk. Felton waved cheerfully. "See ya!" The car pulled smokily away.

The house was dark but Margaret was in her crib and, amazingly, Bree was asleep. It must have been a rough day; usually she was up till two. I undressed as quietly as I could and climbed under the covers beside her. Bree is modest about everything but bed; as long as I've known her she's slept in the nude. It was wonderful cuddling up against her hot skin after that ride in the Bobsled from Hell. In just a few moments I was drifting off myself.

"Richard?" Bree said drowsily.

"That's me."

"Who brought you home?"

I kissed the back of her neck. "Nobody...just one of your fans..."

"Oh," she said, asleep again. And after a minute I joined her.

25

LIE LIKE A WOMAN

CHAPTER THREE

"Picky up? Picky up?" Margaret cried.

I'd been struggling with my tie while she clung tenaciously to my leg, and I was beginning to feel desperate. Bree was putting my breakfast on the table. I looked over at her helplessly. "What does she *want*?"

"She wants you to pick her up."

I looked down at Margaret. "Honey, Daddy doesn't have time to pick you up--"

"PICKY UP!" she screamed. She was relentless. Finally I gave in, scooping Margaret up with one arm as I tried to shovel down some eggs with the other. It was hopeless. Margaret kept cramming her picture book in my face.

"Read? Read book? Read *Bugs Bunny*?" I rolled my eyes, on the verge of hysteria. Bree luckily noticed this and took Margaret from my arms in the nick of time. "Come on, sweetie. Daddy's busy this morning."

Margaret gave me her most cherubic smile. Her strawberry blonde hair was inundated with egg but she still looked like a Botticelli angel. I smiled back. Bree took Margaret into the living room and turned on "Sesame Street". I was just finishing up my toast when she came back.

"Busy day?"

"Yeah. Dad's seeing Tracy this morning and he wants me there for moral support. What are you going to do today?"

"I'm going to buy a car."

I was putting on my jacket, hoping to make a quick getaway, but that remark stopped me short.

"You're *what*?"

"I'm going to buy a car. I got a royalty check." Bree said it casually, as if buying a car was something she did every day.

"I don't understand. You don't believe in having more than one car."

"I do now."

"But--*why*?" I know I must have had a pleading note in my voice at this point. Bree put on her enigmatic look.

"I need one." Case closed. I could tell by the way she was looking at me that this wasn't something she wished to debate. Without a doubt by the time I got home tonight there would be a new car parked in the driveway.

What could I say? It was her money.

"There's no room in the garage."

Bree shrugged, as if garaging a car was the least of her worries. "I'll park it in the street."

"Why can't you just use the Mustang? Take me to work if you want to."

Bree turned and smiled at me ironically. "Am I mistaken or haven't you been wanting me to get another car for the last five years?"

She had me there. Ever since we'd gotten married and she'd sold her Jeep, I'd felt inconvenienced. I hated having her drive my car. It isn't that she's not a good driver--on the contrary, she's cautious to the point of absurdity. But something about the way she shifts gears grates on my nerves. And she was always taking it out and washing it. I keep telling her that those commercial car washes damage the finish, but she hates the way dust looks against the black paint.

She smiled, kissing my cheek. "Don't worry about it, Richard, we can afford it. And I promise I won't come home with anything you'd be ashamed to have parked in front of our house."

Actually, I *had* been a little worried. Her Jeep had been a thirty-year old leftover from some foreign war, not one of the snazzy new four-wheelers you see in the best places. I thought she and Felton had probably bought their cars from the same dealer.

I gave up. "I suppose you want me to take the afternoon off and drive you around."

She was silent for a moment. "Actually, Charlie promised he'd pick me up. He has something to tell me about that skeleton anyway, so he said he'd pick me up and afterward we could look for a car..."

"Oh." I said. I felt my face begin to burn. "Well." I slipped on my coat and stumbled toward the front door, tripping over Margaret's least favorite stuffed bear.

Bree frowned at me. "Are you upset?"

I shrugged. "Me? Why should I be upset?"

She smiled, reassured. "Okay. Have a nice day."

* * *

Dolores Zapata was waiting in the outer office when I arrived at work that morning. She and Rita were talking a mile a minute in Spanish. That's another reason I disapproved of Rita--no matter who came into the office, she could converse with him in his native tongue, no small feat in a city as culturally diversified as San Diego. Why wasn't she working for the United Nations? I couldn't figure out why a woman with her brains and obvious talents would settle for secretarial work with a small-time agency. Something just wasn't right...

"There you are! Why didn't you call me?" Delores yelled as I walked by Rita's desk. She hustled me into my office and slammed the door, obviously furious. She weighed a good three hundred pounds on the hoof and she was solid, so it didn't take much hustling on her part; I wasn't about to object.

"Wha'd am I paying you for? Two months and you don't come up with nothing!"

I cleared my throat. "These things take time."

"Time my *ass*! My sister she called me last night, says she saw Fred at the Sierra Bowl not a week ago."

I was surprised. "Did he have the twins with him?"

Dolores smirked. "No sir he did not! He was with some frowzy blonde as usual, Mr. Detective! Now I'd like to know why you couldn't find *that* out."

I sat down at my desk, looking a great deal more casual than I felt. I have to admit, Dolores intimidated me. She looked every bit as psychopathic as her handsome sons, and I regretted taking the case in the first place.

"That couldn't possibly have been your husband she saw, Mrs. Zapata. I'm sure it was a case of mistaken identity. My operatives assure me that Mr. Zapata left San Diego at the same time the boys disappeared, and my operatives are never wrong."

Dolores looked uncertain. "I dunno..."

I led her to the door. "Go home, Mrs. Zapata. I'll call you when we find out something."

"You better..." she said darkly. "I keep warning you, them twins is *dangerous*. Best they be back with their mother."

"I know, I know..." I soothed. As gently as I could, I pushed her through the waiting room and out into the hall. "We'll take care of it..." She ignored me and tromped down the hall toward the elevator, no doubt caught up in her vision of motherly love as ultimate salvation. I shut the door with a sigh of relief and turned to see Rita smiling at me, shaking her head.

"What?" I said irritably.

"Tracy's on her way up."

I had forgotten. In my depression over Bree's new purchase I had somehow managed to block out the fact today was the day Tracy was coming to see Dad.

"What time?"

She checked her clock. "Twenty minutes."

"Can I get out of it?"

She smiled sweetly. "Not a chance." Of course she was enjoying this. She loved to see me uncomfortable.

I went into my office and dialed home. To my surprise, Bree answered. I didn't really expect her to; I was prepared to hang up when the answering machine came on, and now I didn't know what to say.

"Hello?...Hello?..."

I could tell she was about to hang up. I groped for words.

30

"...hi..."

"*Richard? Is that you? You sound strangled.*"

I cleared my throat again. "Sorry, I must be catching a cold."

"*Is anything the matter?*"

"No...how is the baby?"

"*Fine. She's in the backyard trying to bury the neighbor's cat in the sandbox.*"

"Is it dead?"

"*No.*"

"Like mother, like daughter." That sounded stupid. I paused.

"*Richard, are you all right? You seem tense.*"

"How come don't you call me 'Rick' like everyone else?" I said peevishly.

I could almost feel a cool blast of wind from the receiver. "*All right. I will. Are you done now?*"

I felt a little ashamed. I actually loved the fact that she called me Richard, I was just being mean.

"Yes."

"*Good. Call me again when you really want to talk.*" *Click.*

I listened to the dial tone for a few seconds and then hung up. This day was getting worse and worse. And Tracy wasn't even here yet.

Tracy is my older sister, my only sibling, and the one person in the world I feel most ill-at-ease around. Maybe it's because when we were children Tracy could do everything better than I could. Maybe it's because she still *can.* Or maybe it's because she constantly reminds me of that fact. When I flunked out of law school, she'd just graduated first in her class. She'd gone to work for the district attorney's office and it hadn't been long before she was juggling her own private practice. I'd struggled along for years before Dad had finally taken me into the firm, and Tracy always says to this day, rightly enough, that if it hadn't been for Dad I would still be on the street.

What's funny is that she says it with absolutely no malice-- she disapproves of everyone, regardless, and is the only person around who actually has the audacity to disapprove of Bree, however mildly. The person she disapproves of most, though, is my father, who, due to an inherent weakness of character, had left my mother when Tracy and I were teenagers to live with a cocktail waitress half his age. Of course it hadn't worked out. The fact that my mother had completely forgiven my father and had gone on to a more successful life with a handsome tennis pro has little bearing on Tracy's feelings for Dad, and once a month she comes by, ostensibly to cement their relationship, but actually to berate him for a mistake he made twenty-five years ago and still regrets. He always likes to have me around as a buffer on these days. I hate it, but what can I do? Tracy's been bossing me around for years, and now she's trying to boss around my Dad. *The old guy deserves a break*, I tell myself. *You should be happy to help him out.*

So I sifted through my telephone messages, looking for something, anything, that would get me out of the office today. The only possibility was the message from Charlie left over from yesterday, and I happened to know that Charlie had plans for this afternoon.

I decided to call Bree back, but this time I got the machine and I hung up without leaving a message. I knew Bree wasn't angry. Bree never got angry. She didn't pay enough attention to be angry, or else she was the most forgiving person in the world, I didn't know which. It occurred to me that after five years of marriage I ought to know, but I had to admit that, in a lot of ways, Bree was still a mystery to me. Charlie told me once that if I wanted to know who Bree really was all I had to do was read one of her novels, but somehow I'd never gotten up the nerve. Maybe I was afraid I'd find out something I didn't want to know. As it was, we got on famously. Because she was so easygoing she was wonderful to live with for the most part, and I've always hated upsetting apple carts. I figured that when I married it would be for life, regardless. Somehow the image of a daughter as relentless and vengeful as Tracy making my old age miserable was enough to make me crave monogamy. I was lucky to find Bree; despite her quirks, she was easy and forgiving and supportive and all the things I'd ever wanted in a wife. Unfortunately she'd been married before and was therefore (in Tracy's eyes, at least) not the best candidate for a lifetime commitment. But by the time I'd found she'd been married before, and worse yet, to my best friend, I was already in love with her.

I buzzed Rita and asked her to bring me a cup of coffee. She ignored me. It didn't matter. Twenty minutes later I was sitting at a table at the Snow Panda Restaurant at Horton Plaza, listening to my sister upbraid my father for ruining her junior prom by walking out on Mother while I downed a Mai Tai and wished I were anywhere but here…

* * *

"Did you hear what she *said?*" Dad had on his hangdog look and not even the sight of Rita's legs in sheer black stockings could lift his spirits. He passed by her as if she were a hat stand and went into his office glumly, reaching into the top drawer for the whiskey flask he kept there. When I was a kid I'd assumed he kept whiskey in it; later I'd learned that he kept it full of Pepto-Bismol for just such occasions as this. Apparently my mother had given him her share of these occasions and he had given up drinking long ago in favor of ulcers. Now he took a swig from the bottle, foregoing the spoon, obviously very upset. He was used to Tracy's berating; that wasn't the source of his anguish. Rather, it was her announcement that she was planning to run for District Attorney, and his conviction that she was bound to win if she ran, since she'd never lost a contest in her life.

He was most upset about the fact that Leroy McNaughton, his lifelong friend and current District Attorney, would certainly not forgive him if his daughter beat him out of his office. It was Leroy's view that children should be drowned at birth, particularly girl children, and apparently at the time of Tracy's birth he'd offered to personally drop her off the Coronado ferry. Perhaps Tracy had heard this story told one too many times at the cocktail parties my father used to have in his pre-ulcer days; at any rate, she seemed determined that San Diego law enforcement needed new blood, and she was just the woman for the job. Probably she *would* win, which would make her even more unbearable than ever. I had no doubt that she'd have no scruples whatsoever about interfering with her own father's business practices if she felt interference was warranted, and Dad was looking weary enough nowadays without *that* hanging over his head. I decided to subtly suggest that maybe now that I was so strongly in control of the family business, it might be a good time for him to consider retiring to Bora Bora. He loved to sail and had been talking about going around the world for a long time; and I was getting a little old to still be working for my father. It seemed like the perfect solution to both our problems.

I was just about to broach the subject when Rita buzzed Dad's office, looking for me.

"Felton called. He says Perry Sinker just jumped off the Coronado Bridge..."

CHAPTER FOUR

Felton was *upset*. I drove through the police block and spotted him right away; he was leaning over the rail, staring down into the water, shielding his eyes with one stubby-fingered hand. I could tell he was upset because he was suddenly extremely conspicuous. Otherwise I never would have noticed him. But tension somehow changed his whole countenance. He seemed to *radiate* tension.

I half-expected to see Charlie there, but then I remembered that Charlie was probably at this very moment shopping for a car with my wife and child and I started feeling a little tense myself. I walked over to Felton and he immediately turned to me, his face a mask of remorse.

"He got away from me! One minute I was right behind him, and the next he was out of his car and over the railing!"

I was amazed to find that he was shaking. I put my hand on his shoulder to calm him, but he kept shivering, looking over the railing now and then as if he expected Perry Sinker to be down there in an inner tube, waving up at him.

"I was with him every second. Every second!" He shook his head as if he couldn't believe it was happening to him. To tell the truth, I couldn't believe it was happening to him either. Felton had always had more luck than he deserved. The last thing I'd expected was to find him shivering on a bridge, staring down into the bay.

"Come on, it's cold up here." The fog was beginning to thicken and I knew the police would give up the search soon--in a few minute you wouldn't even be able to see the surface. I led him to the Mustang and put him in the front seat, then got in on the driver's side. I looked around. "Where's your car?"

He jerked a thumb toward a blue Tempo parked a few yards away. "I always rent something inconspicuous when I'm tailing someone," he said softly.

He seemed to calm down a bit. I turned on the radio. I had it tuned to an oldies station and we listened to "Out in the Country" by Three Dog Night. This seemed to have a soothing effect on Felton. After a while, when he stopped shaking, I asked gently, "What happened?"

He squinted his eyes. "It's weird. It started out so normal. He left Bakersfield's place about ten this morning and I followed him out. He was driving a Porsche, so he was a cinch to tail--those things never have any pick-up."

"Where'd he go?"

"University Towne Center, you know, that shopping center near La Jolla? It's about fifteen minutes from Bakersfield's house."

"You mean he really *does* go to shopping centers?" I shook my head.

"*Did.* Did today, anyway. He went into Robinson's and bought a couple of pair of sox. Argyles. Then he went over to the skating rink and ogled the ice skaters for about half an hour. Know what?"

"What?"

"They were *girl* skaters. And he wasn't watching them with clinical interest, either."

I digested that for a moment. "Did he know you were tailing him?"

Felton looked offended. "Do I look like an amateur to you?"

"Sorry. What happened then?"

He thought about it for a moment, rubbing his jaw. "He left. Got in his car and drove off."

"That's all? He didn't talk to anyone? Didn't make any phone calls?"

"Nope."

"Nothing?"

"Well..." I knew something was coming. Felton notices things no other normal human being would think of as significant that almost always turned out to be just that. "He stepped on a piece of gum..."

"He *what*?"

"A big wad of green gum with the wrapper stuck to it--" he smiled. "He was pissed! He had on brand new Italian loafers and it goo-ed up the sole--he had to scrape it off with his car keys." He snickered. Then he remembered that Sinker had just jumped off the bridge and his mouth turned down. "My God. I'm *heartless*..."

"No you're not, Felton," I said impatiently. "So he didn't make a phone call and he didn't talk to anybody."

"Naw, he just watched those girls skating around in those tiny little skirts and those skintight--"

"Then he left?"

"Yeah. I followed him onto the freeway. He wasn't speeding or anything, just kinda driving leisurely, you know, like he was out on a sunny day enjoying the weather. We got onto the bridge and there's no one on it and next thing I know he pulls over to the side without stopping the engine and he's over the rail before I could even get out of my car!"

"Did you see him hit?"

He shook his head. He was shivering again and I turned on the heater. "By the time I managed to get to the side, he was gone..."

"You didn't see him fall?"

"Nope."

"Did anyone see him fall?"

He shrugged. "I was the only one on the bridge that stopped. I guess no one else noticed. People are always in a hurry nowadays."

He jumped suddenly as a patrolman rapped on the window beside his head. "Oh God..." The patrolman motioned him out of the car. "I gotta go now, Rick. I'll probably have to mention your name. Don't be surprised if they call you."

"I won't..." I said grimly. It didn't matter. That was the least of my problems. I was thinking about what Carl Bakersfield was going to say when I told him that the tail I hired let the love of his life jump off the Coronado Bridge...

CHAPTER FIVE

I didn't have to worry; a raven-haired rookie named Jan Merkle told Carl about his paramour before I had a chance to get back to the office. Carl's cell phone was busy for several hours and when I finally got through to him he informed me in a very cool, deliberate voice that he was stopping payment on the check he had issued the day before and if I had any sense at all I would declare bankruptcy as soon as possible because he intended to sue me, my father, and the firm for every penny we had.

Twenty minutes later I got a call from Tracy, of all people.

"*Just what do you think you're trying to pull, Rick Matthews?*"

I could tell by her tone that she was furious but I hadn't any idea what I'd done to make her that way. "Gee, I don't know. You want me to guess? "

"*I should never have told you that I was running for district attorney! I should have known you'd pull something like this!*"

"Like what, Tracy? Spit it out, I've had a hard day..."

"*I suppose you're trying to tell me that you didn't know my law firm handled Carl Bakersfield's affairs?*"

I almost smiled. "As a matter of fact, I didn't."

"*Well, it turns out that he's adamantine about suing you and Dad, and I don't know how I'm going to keep it out of the papers that we're related! Even if I don't lose Carl as a client, and he's one of the biggest clients I have, I'm bound to look like a fool, and that's not going to help my campaign any!"*

"Is it your contention, Tracy, that I deliberately goaded your client's lover into jumping off a bridge just to hurt your chances in the race for district attorney? Or maybe you just assumed that I arranged for Felton to push him off."

She was silent for a moment. Obviously the thought *had* occurred to her, but it sounded so ludicrous when I said it out loud that she couldn't continue her scolding. "*You could have been more careful,*" she answered sullenly.

"I wasn't there. And Felton is always careful."

She sniffed. "*Felton is a disreputable slob and you had no business hiring him.*"

"If you feel that way about it, Trace, you shouldn't have send Bakersfield over here in the first place."

She barked a short laugh. "*Me? Recommend you? You must be insane.*"

"If I am, it runs in the family," I said shortly, hanging up. I'd never hung up on her before but it made me feel strong and manly to do it and I resolved to make a habit of it. Then I realized that she'd probably take it out on Dad and I started feeling bad again. She must have known that Carl Bakersfield didn't have grounds for a suit and she was just trying to give me a hard time. I tried to remember when I'd gotten big enough that she'd had to stop using her fists to beat me up and start using her tongue, but my memory just wasn't that good.

I decided enough was enough and told Rita I was going home. "If the police department calls, tell them I'm dead."

Rita frowned. "Not funny."

I sighed. "I wasn't trying to be funny. I *am* dead."

"I'll tell them you said that."

* * *

I pulled into the driveway without remembering to look on our street for Bree's new car. Our house is situated in the middle of the block, a modest blue-and-white frame cottage that contrasts sharply with the oversize pink stucco castles on either side of us. Strangely enough, everyone on this block has single car garages and there are always cars lining the street-- everything from Rabbits to Mercedes. Somehow I knew Bree wouldn't bring home a Mercedes; I figured a Rabbit was more her speed. I walked out onto the front sidewalk, trying to figure out which car was hers. None of them looked new enough. I went up to the front door and started trying my keys. It'd been so long since I'd entered through the front door that I couldn't remember which key fit it. Of course Bree's dog, Lester, heard me at the lock and went crazy. I call him Bree's dog because, although we got him the year after we were married, he was strictly Bree's idea.

In the first place, I would never name a dog Lester and in the second place, if I were choosing a dog for myself, I'd go to a pet store or a reputable breeder, not to the city pound to pick out the largest, least trainable mongrel awaiting execution there. Lester was a good one-hundred-and-twenty pounds and as bulky as a St. Bernard, although there the resemblance ended. He looked for all the world like an oversized, overweight, rust-colored poodle with a bulldog's face and the eyes of a ferret. He *terrified* me. The people at the pound had told us that he's been turned in after he had eaten his owner's living room rug. Not chewed it up- -*eaten* it. The entire rug. I suppose they'd thought he might have a discipline problem. They had also neglected to paper-train him, since at the time of his full growth he'd been just six months old. I'd been eyeing a half-dachshund, half-corgi puppy already, but Bree had spotted Lester right away, and had insisted that we take him home. "They'll *kill* him if we don't," she'd said, sticking up for the underdog, as usual. Since she was the one who had to stay home, I'd let her pick the dog, and I've regretted it ever since. Within a month Lester had eaten *our* living room rug, as well as devoured my videotape copy of *It Came from Outer Space*, and once in a fit of enthusiasm he'd broken our dining room table in two by jumping onto it to finish off some English muffins left over from breakfast. I'd wanted to give him back to the pound, but Bree wouldn't hear of it. As far as she was concerned, he was family, and you don't give away a member of the family no matter how destructive he is.

Finally I found the right key and pushed in. Lester, seeing it was me, moved away in disappointment, and I went into the living room and sat down heavily on the sofa. Usually I head back to the kitchen, but tonight I was just too tired. I was about to put my feet up on the coffee table when Bree came up behind me and started rubbing my neck. For a small woman she has remarkably strong hands and she knows just how to use them. I shut my eyes and started to relax.

"Where's your car?" I murmured.

"They had to order it from another dealership..." she said softly, "It won't come in until next week..."

"Where's the baby?"

"At Janie's..." Janie was Bree's best friend and one of the few people with whom she would trust Margaret.

She moved down to my shoulders and I groaned with pleasure. She really knew what she was doing when it came to my shoulders; I discovered early on how much enjoyment she derived from doing this, serving me in small, significant ways, and suddenly I remembered why I had married her. If she were maddening in some ways, she was totally giving in others, and I didn't care if she had twenty ex-husbands and a dozen of delinquent dogs. I grabbed her hand.

"Let's continue this in the bedroom." I turned to her and realized that she was wearing the scarlet silk nightgown Margaret usually carried around with her. It looked better on Bree.

"What's the matter with right here?" She closed the front shutters and moved into my lap and for awhile I completely forgot about Bakersfield and Charlie and Tracy and let Bree's hands do the talking...

* * *

When I woke up, I realized that I was starving. There were clothes strewn from one end of the living room to another. The scarlet silkie was lying behind the sofa, and Bree was gone. The room was completely dark and I sat up and turned on the Japanese lamp behind my head. Bree walked in, wearing my bathrobe and carrying a tray. I shook my head. That was the second time in an hour she'd read my mind.

"What's that?" I asked.

She set the tray down in front of me on the coffee table. "Homemade vegetable soup. Cornbread. Honey butter. Iced tea."

I was ravenous. I immediately began eating enthusiastically, which wasn't difficult considering that Bree cooks better than anyone, even my own mother, who is no slouch. Bree sat down opposite me in the rattan chair and began to nibble on my cornbread, watching me intently, as if she had something on her mind. After a few minutes she spoke.

"I heard about Perry Sinker."

I made a sour face. "Yeah, can you believe it? Felton's in agony. First day out, too."

She looked at me, her mossy eyes unfathomable. A stray curl hung in her face and she shook it back impatiently. "Do you think it was a suicide?"

I frowned. "What else would it be?"

She shrugged. "Murder?"

I scoffed. "Who? Felton? He was the only one there!"

Again she shrugged and I had a feeling she knew something she wasn't telling me. She went back to the kitchen to refill my iced tea glass and I thought about it for a minute. Then I remembered that she'd been with Charlie all afternoon and that it was perfectly possible for her to know something that I didn't. She came back in slowly, my striped velour robe wrapped around her small shoulders, and I marveled that something that looked so sloppy on me could look so elegant on her. She handed me the tea with a smile.

"You must have been hungry."

"I was..." I took a big gulp, then looked at her. "Did Charlie take you car-shopping?"

She nodded. "We got the call on his radio. Did Felton call you?"

"From the bridge."

"Oh..." Again the hesitancy. Then she spoke. "Strange, isn't it, that a skeleton should be discovered in Perry Sinker's rental house just days before Perry decides to end his life? I mean, if I wrote that in a book, people would think it was too coincidental. They'd immediately start looking for a pattern."

"Is that what you're doing?" I asked lightly.

"What?"

"Looking for a pattern."

She looked amused. "It's *your* case."

"Not any more. Carl fired me." I downed the rest of the iced tea and reached for her again. She giggled as I pulled her down on the couch. For such a serious woman, Bree has a remarkably childlike giggle. "So when's Janie bringing Margaret home?" I said into her hair.

"Any minute."

That dampened my ardor considerably and I let her up. She was still looking at me in that funny way.

"What?"

She frowned. "Did you know that Carl Bakersfield was married?"

"What?!"

"Yeah. He got married about four years ago to a debutante he met at some country club function. Her name is Marilyn Cutter. Or was..."

"What do you mean, *was*?"

She shrugged. "Well, apparently she walked out on him several months ago. No one seems to know where she went, not her family, not her friends. Disappeared."

"Did Charlie tell you this?"

She smiled ironically. "Charlie and a few others. I didn't spend all day baking cornbread."

I grabbed my jeans and started climbing into them. It was going to be another cold night. "I'll bet you didn't. And Charlie-- does he think that's Marilyn's skeleton bricked into the wall?"

"It's possible..." She cleared off the dishes and put them on the tray.

I pulled on my shirt and followed her into the kitchen barefooted. She had it decorated in red-and-white and everything looked bright and cheerful even though it was past dark. It was tiny, though; barely room enough for both of us, let alone Lester, who decided that if he were lucky Bree would drop a crumb or two and that under my feet was probably the best place for him to sit.

"Did Carl file a missing person's report?"

She shook her head firmly. "Nope. Apparently he doesn't consider her missing. He says she bought a sailboat and could be anywhere in the South Pacific. She was quite a sailor, belonged to the Coronado sail club. Isn't that the one your dad used to go to?"

"Maybe he knew her."

"I doubt it. She was quite a society lady."

"Are you implying that my father is not high enough on the society ladder to mix with Marilyn Cutter?"

I was kidding but she looked at me and made a face, handing me a cup of steaming cinnamon coffee. She'd gotten it down the street at the Kensington Coffee Company, a tiny combination coffee shop and sidewalk cafe that always smelled like heaven. She and Margaret went past there every day on their way to the park, and when I was really lucky she'd bring home some exotic tea or coffee to test on me before bedtime. "Try this," she said. "It's decaffeinated."

We sat down at the kitchen table. The coffee was scalding and I had to blow on it a minute before I could take a sip. Bree got out some cookies she'd made, chewy things filled with nuts and chocolate chips and cocoanut and calories. I'd warned her that already my waistline was beginning to disappear, but she paid me no mind.

"No wonder Charlie got so fat," I growled, biting into one of the cookies.

She raised an eyebrow. "I never baked for Charlie..."

"Sure. I'll bet."

"No, it's true. If he got fat, he didn't do it at home..." She said this almost sadly and I decided not to pursue it. Besides, I was still thinking about Bakersfield and something was bothering me.

"So how did Charlie find out that Marilyn Cutter was missing? Who filed the report?"

She looked at me in surprise. "I thought I told you. Perry Sinker, of course."

"Perry Sinker filed a missing persons' report on Carl Bakersfield's wife?"

"Right."

"Why?"

She smiled grimly. "I guess we'll never know that now, will we?"

"I could ask Carl. I'll bet he knows."

She cocked her head. "What makes you think he'd tell you? Or even talk to you?"

"I can be very persuasive at times..." I smiled at her.

She smiled back, a sexy Bree smile. "I know..."

I reached for her.

The doorbell rang. Lester went wild.

Bree shrugged. "Baby's home."

I sighed.

CHAPTER SIX

"Bree's looking good these days," Charlie remarked casually.

We were sitting in his office at police headquarters while Felton signed a statement. I had brought Felton down myself. Since the accident, he couldn't be trusted to drive. In fact, he could hardly navigate his way to the bathroom. He was a broken man; all the spirit had gone out of him. I felt sorry for him, and partially responsible. More and more I was beginning to believe that Carl Bakersfield had more to hide than his sexual proclivities.

Charlie was sitting on top of his desk, dangling one foot as he tried to light his pipe. It was one of those bent briar pipes, very tweedy, and for as long as I could remember Charlie had been trying to master it, but it continued to smolder and burn out stubbornly every time he tried to light it. Finally he settled for just holding it in his mouth. "She looks good with her hair long like that," he said through his teeth. "Pretty."

"Yeah," I said, trying to sound just as casual and failing. Where Bree is concerned I have a hard time being casual. It irks me when Charlie speaks so knowledgeably about my wife. Of course later when I analyze it, I can see that he never really says anything out of line, but at the time it burns my ass.

I looked around Charlie's office. It was in perfect order, a place for everything and everything in its place. Books lined up on shelves according to size and color, papers properly stacked, bulletin board bereft of litter. The ancient walnut desk smelled as though it had just been polished; each pen and pencil was neatly contained in a cup with the initial W for Waxman. A brass name plate that said: CHARLES M. WAXMAN, LIEUTENANT, stood exactly three inches from the edge of the desk. It was *always* exactly three inches from the edge of the desk. It occurred to me that it might be glued there and I surreptitiously nudged it with my elbow. It moved over half an inch. Charlie casually reached down and automatically moved it back exactly three inches from the edge of the desk. He looked up at me again, smiling broadly.

"What about lunch? I found this great bar in Mission Valley; the waitresses dress up in poodle skirts and bouffants," he said happily.

"I don't know," I replied. "I've got a lot of running around to do today. Besides, poodle skirts were a little before my time. My taste runs more to mini-skirts."

"You're covered!" Charlie grinned. "They're mini-poodle skirts! Two decades for the price of one!" He blew out imaginary smoke. "So, how's Tracy?"

I sighed. Of course Bree had told Charlie I was seeing Tracy yesterday; why shouldn't she?

"She's Tracy, as usual," I said. Charlie had made the mistake of trying to date Tracy before she married Maynard, her steely-eyed husband, and he'd soon found out why I complained about her so constantly. Actually, Tracy is a fairly attractive woman if you subtract her personality. She has great legs, and there'd been a time, before my dad left home, when she'd been considered fun-loving. Charlie had tried taking her roller skating once. She'd fractured an ankle; she'd been in a cast for months. She's never let me forget it.

The door opened and Felton skulked in, head down. Charlie gave him a hearty slap on the shoulder, wringing his hand. Felton winced. Charlie was easily twice his size, and in his present condition Felton was hardly a match for a Chihuahua.

"Done?" I asked Felton. He nodded, standing silently. Charlie shot me a quizzical look, but I ignored it. "Come on, Felton, I'll take you home." He nodded again, barely looking up. Charlie guided us to the door. "Have a nice day!" he shouted as we left.

* * *

"How's Felton?" Rita asked as I walked into the reception room. It was unlike her to show an interest in Felton and I was oddly touched.

"He'll live," I said briefly. "Dad in yet?"

Rita shook her black waves. "He called in sick." She got up from her desk and followed me into my office. She was fond of red and today she sported a scarlet dress as bright as a stoplight. "I think being sued makes him bilious."

"It always has that effect on *me*," I said, sitting down behind my desk on my lousy straight-back chair. I was determined to fill the office with comfortable chairs just as soon as Dad retired.

Rita frowned at me. I could tell she had something on her mind. Why is it that women never come right out with anything? You always have to ask.

I bit. "What is it, Rita?"

"I've been doing a little research on your friend Carl Bakersfield."

"Research? What kind of research?"

"You know, the usual. Tax forms, residential records, credit reports. I was curious."

"About what?"

She raised an eyebrow. "About why a loser like Perry Sinker would want to commit suicide when he was set for life with a sugar daddy as rich and powerful as Bakersfield."

I shrugged. "Could be a lot of reasons. Could be Perry thought he couldn't keep Carl on the line much longer--after all, he was almost thirty."

"Possible, but doubtful. With his record he doesn't impress me as being the kind of guy who would give up easily...and there's always palimony."

"Well, maybe Perry really *did* have a secret lover, and his love was unrequited."

"With those dimples? *Ha*!"

49

I put my feet up on my desk confidently. "Okay, try this one on for size. Maybe Perry murdered Mrs. Carl Bakersfield and buried her skeleton in the wall of his two-bedroom on Adams and he knew that it was just a matter of time till we sent him up to Sing-Sing."

Rita smiled then, flashing those dazzling teeth. "Ah, you know about the wife, then."

"Bree told me."

"I don't doubt it. She should be the detective in the family." She moved over to a folder on my desk and opened it, pulling out the eight-by-ten of Perry Sinker that Carl had so generously provided. She stared hard at the photo. "I wonder when this was taken..."

"What difference does it make?"

"Probably none. What makes you think Perry killed Mrs. Bakersfield?"

"I don't think he killed her; I just said it was a *possibility*. After all, he and Carl were lovers before Carl met Marilyn Cutter and married her. He was jealous, as well he should be. Motive enough for murder, I'd say."

"But not for *suicide*...How's the baby?"

"She's fine," I said, irritated with her for changing the subject. "But she didn't kill Marilyn Cutter. Though I'm not saying she's incapable of it."

Rita stared at the eight-by-ten. "No one killed Marilyn Cutter," she murmured thoughtfully.

"What do you mean?"

"Her father died last Sunday. Marilyn attended the funeral yesterday..." She threw me a clipping from the San Diego Chronicle. There, in glorious black-and-white, was a photograph from Sebastian Cutter's funeral, clearly showing a busty blonde woman in a black veil standing between two young men at grave side.

The caption read:

CUTTER CHILDREN ATTEND FATHER'S FUNERAL.
THREE WILL SHARE FIFTY MILLION DOLLAR ESTATE

Rita gazed at me. "Not exactly skeletal, is she?"

I grabbed my jacket and Rita's hand. "Let's go find out."

* * *

I should have known that getting into the Cutter Mansion was easier said than done, particularly the day after Mr. Cutter's funeral.

The place was swarming with guards. Two stood outside the eight-foot-high stucco wall that surrounded the place, and through the cast iron gate I could see three or four others milling around the front entrance as if they'd been hired for the occasion and weren't quite sure of their duties.

"Why all the guards?" Rita asked suspiciously. We were in her car, a bright red Cutlass with matching leather upholstery. It smelled brand new, and when I got into the car I noticed that her bumper sticker said "SHIT HAPPENS." I forgot to ask her what the hell that meant. I was too knocked out by the car itself. It must have cost her more than I paid her in a year, and it made me realize just how little I knew about Rita's personal life.

Rita pulled up to the gate carefully. One of the guards came over as she rolled down the window. She smiled her best smile, one guaranteed to knock a smirk off an ordinary guy's lips at twenty paces, but this gorilla was oblivious. Or maybe the sun was in his eyes.

"Whadaya want?" he grunted.

"I'm here to see Marilyn Cutter," Rita said, still smiling determinedly.

The gorilla shook his head. He was as large as a sumo wrestler and his collar was at least two sizes too small, giving the impression that his head had been squeezed out of his neck like a glob of toothpaste. "She ain't here. Scram."

I waited for Rita to roll up her window and turn the car around, but she didn't. Instead she widened her smile and said softly, so that the guard would have to bend down to hear her, "Of course she's here. She just called and asked me to come over."

The gorilla squinted at Rita. "I *tole* you she ain't here, lady. Get lost!"

Now Rita's eyes began flashing. Her smile slowly disappeared and what replaced it gave me a chill. She reached up with one vermilion-clawed hand and grabbed the gorilla's tie, yanking it tight till his eyes bulged. With his face just an inch away from hers, she hissed in a voice that could crack crystal, "Listen, you *fungus*! I happen to be Miss Cutter's personal masseuse and she is *tense*! She is *so* tense that if she doesn't get a massage immediately she's liable to run amok and fire everyone on the premises. In fact, she may even hold a grudge and I understand that this family has connections to the Mafia so if you don't want to end up with a bloody horse head under your pillow *you'll open that goddamn gate and LET ME IN!*" She screamed this last part and pulled tighter on the tie. The gorilla was so confounded that he immediately reached behind him and pushed a green button. The gate parted like the Red Sea. Rita let go of his tie and smiled her prom queen smile once more.

"Thank you so *very* much," she said politely, stomping on the gas. We shot through the gate, spraying gravel directly at the unfortunate red-faced guard behind us.

I stared at Rita. "Something I learned from my mother, God rest her soul," she said, as she pulled up smoothly in front of the entrance. I stepped out, forgetting to open her door. She probably wouldn't have liked it anyway; Rita is nothing if not liberated. She got out on her own and we trotted up the steps.

The Cutter Mansion was all stucco and tile, beautifully embellished with exotic vegetation. It looked more like an old Spanish mission than a home; there was a sense of history about it. The guards didn't bother to stop us, although I noticed several of them standing stock still, staring at Rita's red dress. We slipped through the front door into a huge marble foyer with a sprawling curved staircase smack in the middle of it the size of a football bleacher.

"Somehow I doubt if they've labeled the rooms according to contents," Rita remarked dryly. "How are we going to find her?"

"Good question," I replied, stymied. Despite the overabundance of outside help, there wasn't a sign of a house servant anywhere. I expected at the very least Sir Arthur Gielgud in a monkey suit, but we couldn't even raise a chambermaid.

"Now if only we had our Dick Tracy two-way wrist radios, I could look downstairs and you could look upstairs and--"

"Right," I said shortly, sick as usual of Rita's sarcasm. I shoved her off to the left and started up the stairs without her. "If you find her, whistle. You do know how to whistle, don't you?"

Rita smiled. "Of course. You're supposed to put your lips together and blow...but I do it like this." And amazingly, she stuck two fingers in her mouth and let out a piercing screech that shook the chandelier. I stared at her in astonishment.

"What the hell are you *doing*?"

"Trying to find out if anybody's home." We stood for a moment, waiting. Nothing. I waved Rita on. "Don't do that again!" I hissed. She laughed and disappeared though a pair of enormous black lacquered doors.

I started up the curved staircase, pausing at the top, unable to make up my mind whether to go right or left. Not a huge decision, but lately I'd had a lot on my mind and little things seemed to loom impossible. I listened for a moment and thought I heard running water. A toilet flushing, maybe? It was worth an investigation. I turned right and started down a long carpeted hallway. On either side of me the walls were covered with rich brocade and original paintings by the masters. At least I think they were original—art history wasn't exactly my forte, but they looked real enough. The ceiling was at least fifteen feet high and despite the fact that I was wearing gum-soled Bass Weejums, my footfalls echoed on the polished hardwood floor. It was eerie; I felt a little uneasy as I opened the first door on my left and peered inside.

It was a bedroom, a woman's bedroom, from what I could tell, with a large, elegant four-poster in one corner and a dressing table across from the window. There were pink gauze curtains that let in just enough sunlight to see but not enough to see clearly, and lined up against one of the walls were walnut bookshelves filled to overflowing with paperbacks. They seemed so out of sync with this classic decor that I stepped over and reached up, taking a couple off the top shelf. The covers were different but basically alike: a woman in a low-cut satin ball gown, bosom heaving, being bent backward by a tall, dark, handsome stranger, sometimes with a mustache, sometimes not. The titles were great: *Passion of the Gods*, *Love's Savage Flame*, etc. Romances. My mother-in-law checked them out of the library by the dozens, but I'd always associated them with bored Midwestern housewives. Apparently you didn't have to be a Midwestern housewife to be bored.

On the dressing table in a gold frame was a picture of three small children at a recital. It was black-and-white, two little boys and a slightly older blonde girl in glasses. I thought I saw Marilyn Cutter in that little girl, and as I picked up the photo I heard a smooth, deep voice behind me.

"I've never seen a burglar in a suit and tie--" it said languidly, *"--but perhaps you're trying to start a trend..."*

I turned slowly. Marilyn Cutter was standing there in an ice blue dressing gown, her thick pale hair falling to her shoulders. She was beautiful, certainly; not as busty as I'd first thought, but stunning nonetheless. Her skin was a golden tan and her eyes almost black, heavily made up and stern. In fact, her whole countenance was stern and disapproving. But nothing had prepared me for the fact that she was at least as tall as I was.

And she was pointing a gun at me.

"I've always wondered if shooting an intruder in your own home constituted manslaughter or self-defense..."

I held up my empty hands. "I'm unarmed, see? It'd definitely be manslaughter. Maybe even second degree murder."

She didn't smile. "I might like prison," she said thoughtfully, her voice dark and husky. "No responsibilities, no intrusions, no...*men*."

I cleared my throat uneasily. "You'd lose your tan," I said steadily.

She cocked her head, considering. Then she raised her gun and aimed. "It might be worth it..." she murmured, closing a tapered finger over the trigger. I shut my eyes.

"DADDY!!" screamed a high tiny voice. I opened them just in time to see Margaret as she tackled my knees violently. Marilyn lowered the gun. I was totally confused.

54

"Margaret, what the hell--?" I looked up as Bree stepped through the doorway. She raised her eyebrows. Marilyn turned and looked at her.

"I take it you know this prowler," she said to Bree.

I kneeled down and Margaret scrambled into my arms.

"It's Daddy!" she said gleefully. Bree frowned at me, the same way she always frowned at me when I interrupted her while she was writing. "I know him," she said abruptly. "Intimately."

"Well," said Marilyn, disappointed. She was looking rather regretfully at Bree, and I couldn't tell whether she was frustrated because she didn't know Bree was married, or because she had really wanted to shoot me.

We stood around staring at each other for a moment silently. The door to the adjoining bathroom opened suddenly and out came an elderly lady with bluish hair. She wore a ruffled pink negligee. In one hand was a half-eaten chocolate, in the other a worn paperback with a picture of a half-clad woman being embraced by a tall, handsome, well-muscled man. The poor woman jumped when she saw us, considerably startled. I felt sorry for her. After all, all she'd done was gone to the bathroom.

"It's all right, Mother," said Marilyn, sighing resignedly. "We were just leaving..."

LIE LIKE A WOMAN

CHAPTER SEVEN

Margaret sat on my lap, twisted at the waist, so that her little round face was planted squarely in front of my big square one. She had her sticky fingers clasped firmly to my nose. "I got your nose!" she giggled gleefully, digging in her sharp little nails. She pulled as hard as she could, then stuck her fingers in her mouth. "See, I *ate* it!" She gulped a pronounced gulp and opened her mouth wide so that I could see it was empty. "See, Daddy? *See*?"

I smiled thinly. "I see." I was in the back seat; in the front seat Bree and Rita were having a semi-heated discussion on the merits of John Updike's prose. It seemed like every time they got together, they discussed literature or art or something that seemed specifically designed to make me feel like a dunderhead. I wasn't uneducated, but my interests ran more to things that didn't involve deep personal angst. I had enough angst of my own to not be entertained by reading about someone else's.

Rita drove wildly even on her best days, and with Bree in her ear it seemed as if all her concentration were drained away.

"Watch out for that truck!" I shouted as we careened into the left lane on a highway already crammed with homeward bound GI's.

"I see it, Rick. Don't be so nervous." Rita swerved gently, barely missing the truck. "You're just upset because your wife beat you to the draw, as usual," she said, looking over the back seat to smirk at me.

"Keep your eye on the road!" I looked out the window at downtown, thinking how crowded San Diego had become over the past five years. All that building in the valley had done it. Used to be you could go out in the middle of the day and hardly see another car. Now it was bumper-to-bumper from morning to night.

"I fail to understand how getting in to see Marilyn Cutter is beating me to the draw," I said sullenly to Rita, "--but since you mention it--" I turned to Bree, "--just how *did* you get past those guards?"

Bree blushed. She has fine pale skin with a scattering of freckles across the bridge of her nose, and she's given to blushing at the slightest provocation.

"I gave them each a copy of my new book..." she said demurely, "...apparently they all know Joshua Brood..."

Rita hooted. I felt the skin at the nape of my neck prickling.

"At any rate I didn't get very far. She wasn't anxious to expose herself to someone who's doing an article for *The Reader* on the skeleton in her husband's lover's house..."

"Who told her that?"

"I did."

"Why?"

"Because I am."

I looked at her incredulously. "You're doing an article for *The Reader*? On my case?"

"You said it wasn't your case anymore," Bree answered logically.

"You don't write articles!"

She looked at me innocently. "I was asked to. Daniel Harwood called me personally."

I sulked in the backseat. When we reached the office, Rita let me out. "I'll just run Bree home," she said happily, pulling out into the street right in front of a furiously honking Mercedes. I stood there on the sidewalk, feeling as if my life were getting completely out of hand.

It was about to get worse. As I stepped onto the elevator, a sleaze ball in a black tattered vest handed me a summons to appear at an inquest investigating the death of Perry Sinker.

CHAPTER EIGHT

Felton looked out at me from under heavy eyelids. Since the suicide, he'd consistently appeared to be coming down with a bad case of flu.

"You want *me* to meet Bree's parents' plane?"

"Sorry, Felton, but I have a summons to appear in court this afternoon at Perry Sinker's inquest."

Felton looked hurt. "I didn't get a summons."

"No doubt you will. In the meantime, can't you do this one little favor for me?"

His voice was barely a whisper. "Can't Bree do it?"

"No, she can't. It's supposed to be a surprise for her birthday. C'mon, Felton, what are you afraid of?"

He turned his head away, too late to hide the tears welling up in his eyes.

"Blowing it..."

I put an arm around his shoulder. "Buck up, kid, you won't blow it. There's no one I have more faith in than you." I was really worried about Felton. He hardly ate enough to keep a pigeon alive. and his appearance, which had always been somewhat disheveled, was now on the public shelter level. Even hard-hearted Rita had invited him to have dinner with her out of pity, but Felton, who in the old days would have eaten shoe leather just to get within ten feet of those dangerous curves, could only shake his head sadly and walk away.

We were sitting in my office, Felton curled up fetally in one of the stuffed clients' chairs, me badly positioned behind my desk, my ass sore, as usual. I glanced out the window, which was four stories up, and could just make out a fog bank moving in over the bay. It was *cold*. I couldn't remember an October in San Diego that had been this cold, and I'd lived here all my life. Felton had three coats on, layered, like he expected to have to sleep in the train yard in sub-zero weather. The building we were occupying was built in the twenties and had been renovated recently, but the heating system was still archaic and my hands were stiff with cold. Naturally Bree's parents, who had never visited us in the five years we'd been married, picked the coldest October on the record books to make an appearance. Somehow it didn't surprise me.

"Okay," Felton said suddenly. I had almost forgotten he was there. "I'll pick them up. What do they look like?"

I took a Polaroid out of my desk drawer, one we took five Christmases ago at their house, of Bree sitting beside Hugo and Helen in their living room with their hateful dachshund, Waffles, plopped in her lap. Bree had grown up with dachshunds and this fact had no doubt given her *her* taste for obnoxious dogs. I hated Waffles. He bit me on the ear the first time we met and thereafter decided that the only thing I was good for was sharpening his teeth, and he attempted to sharpen his teeth on me every time I saw him.

I handed the snapshot to Felton and sent him on his way. We were only about ten minutes from the airport, but I didn't want to take any chances.

Felton looked at the Polaroid thoughtfully for a minute. "Cute dog," he said, without a hint of sarcasm in his voice. Then, as he turned to leave, he said, without looking at me, "Do you think I'll be indicted in Perry's death?"

I was astounded. "What for? You didn't do anything!"

"That's what I mean. For not doing anything."

"Felton, it wasn't your fault! If it's anyone's fault, it's Carl Bakersfield's, for not letting us know that Sinker was suicidal."

Felton sighed deeply. "Maybe you're right..." he said, obviously unconvinced, as he went out, shutting the door softly behind him.

"Bye, Felton," I heard Rita say, but he just grunted and kept walking.

LIE LIKE A WOMAN

CHAPTER NINE

The hearing was at two o'clock in the federal building downtown, which is barely walking distance from my office. Unfortunately our cold snap hadn't let up and the sky was filled with black, threatening clouds, the kind that are common in Chicago but alien in Southern California. What *was* this? Naturally I wasn't wearing an overcoat--the only one I had was the one I bought when we went to Kansas City last Christmas, and it was the general size and weight of a buffalo hide. I pulled my jacket close and shivered as I jogged toward the courthouse. In the square the homeless were huddled under newspapers, looking a little more put upon than usual. No one hit me up for change today; it was just too cold to bother.

I knew the bailiff from way back and I stopped to talk to him for a minute. His name was Mel Farley and he was known as a character. He was about three feet tall and smoked the most noxious cigars you can imagine, but the judges put up with him because he was a terrific storyteller. He could put you on the edge of your seat for five minutes and finish with a punchline that would have tears running down your face every time you thought of it, and they kept him around purely for entertainment's sake, because frankly, as a bailiff he lacked authority.

Mel had just finished telling me a story about two senators and an alligator that had me wheezing despite the seriousness of my circumstances when Carl Bakersfield walked in. He eyed me coldly, as if whatever I had might be catching and that it was my own fault I had it, and then motioned behind him. He was followed by Marilyn Cutter, a towering Amazon in five-inch spiked heels and hair at least that high. She didn't seem to recognize me, but then, she wasn't looking. She was engaged in intimate conversation with, of all people, my sister Tracy, who toted her Oscar de la Renta briefcase as if it grew out of the end of her arm. Tracy spotted me and gave me an even dirtier look than Carl had and I quit laughing and shivered again. They passed in majestic silence and entered the courtroom through swinging doors.

Mel looked after them thoughtfully. "You know that babe?" he said to me.

"My sister..." I mumbled.

Mel raised an eyebrow. "Nice legs."

"Yeah."

"That reminds me of a story..."

* * *

I was ten minutes late when I finally pulled away from Mel and sat down in the hearing room. Dad had been subpoenaed too, but he was still feeling poorly and had a doctor's excuse. I wasn't that lucky. For fifty minutes I was grilled by the assistant D.A., Simon Wischerath, a candidate for the Perry Mason School of melodramatics if there ever was one. Actually, Simon wasn't a bad guy if you took him out of the courtroom. We'd played Frisbee golf over at Balboa Park a couple of times and he's fairly relaxed ordinarily, but there's something about a judge and a jury box that sets him off. I didn't know how many ways I could say that I didn't know why Perry jumped, and something about the way Simon kept implying that it might somehow be my fault rattled me. I think Tracy must have put a bug in his ear. At any rate it was over in an hour and I didn't stick around. Carl Bakersfield had just fixed me with the evil eye and when I saw Tracy get up and head my way, grim determination on her face, I got out of there.

On my way out Mel caught me by the arm and said, "I hear they're gonna string up your pal tomorrow."

"What pal? You mean Felton?"

Mel nodded sagely, chewing his big cigar with vigor. "They wanna strip him of his license, from what I hear. That big blond billionaire's behind it. Him and his fancy lady lawyer."

"Really..." The way Felton had been acting lately, I wouldn't be surprised if he confessed to first degree murder and begged for the gas chamber out of sheer guilt. I could just imagine what Simon Wischerath and his courtroom tactics would do to poor Felton. As much as I dreaded it, I knew I would have to call Tracy and plead tolerance for Felton; otherwise he might fall apart completely.

"Thanks for the info, Mel."

He tipped his hat. "No problem, Chief. That reminds me of a story..."

* * *

When I got home, no one was there except Lester, who greeted me without enthusiasm, then went patiently back to the door to wait. Bree had left a note saying that she and the baby had gone to Janie's, but there wasn't a trace of Felton or Bree's parents. I called the airport. The plane had arrived on time, and Bree's folks had disembarked, carrying their obnoxious dachshund in an airline carrying case, but no one could tell me if they had been picked up, and if so, by whom. I started imagining what could have happened: they'd taken Felton for a kidnapper and had fled into the path of an oncoming cab; or maybe Felton's disreputable car had broken down a few blocks away in Normal Heights and they'd gone to a neighborhood grocery to phone me, only to be interrupted by an armed robber who'd taken offense at their Midwestern accents and had shot them dead on the spot. Actually, that wasn't too farfetched: lately there'd been a rash of daytime robberies in Normal Heights, which was only a few short blocks from here, and I'd been pushing Bree to start looking for another rental, or maybe even to buy a house, now that we'd been married five years. I was in the middle of a fantasy about Helen and Hugo being so appalled by Felton's appearance that they'd had him arrested by the airport guards when the three of them pulled up in the driveway.

Felton got out of the Bobsled from Hell and Waffles, the dachshund, jumped joyfully into his arms. I came out to help Helen and Hugo, but apparently they were already familiar with the idiosyncrasies of Felton's car; I saw Helen reach out a well-shod foot and spring the front door with one swift kick. Felton saw me and looked sheepish suddenly, but Helen and Hugo were all smiles.

"Here we are!" Helen cried gaily. She was dressed in a print sundress that was entirely too flimsy for the weather we'd been having, and she looked more than a little disheveled, but her spirits were still determinedly high. "Where's that darling grandbaby of mine?"

"Your guess is as good as mine," I said, taking her bag. Felton stood there cuddling the dog and grinning like a fool. Hugo managed to haul his two hundred pound, six-foot-two inch frame out of the backseat and he came over and wrung my hand enthusiastically. "How are ya, Rick?" he boomed. He turned to Felton and slapped him on the back. "Great little guy you sent for us here! Took us on a tour of the city! Bit cooler than I thought it'd be!" Hugo always talked as if he were running for office and had to reach the back row. He was a good guy, but loud. I backed away a bit.

"It's just *wonderful*!" said Helen. "I told Felton here, I told him, it's every bit as beautiful as Brendalee says it is! We just love it, don't we, Daddy?"

Felton looked puzzled. "Brendalee? Who's Brendalee?"

"It's a long story," I said to Felton abruptly, irritated in this sudden change in his demeanor. I knew Bree would kill me if I told him how she'd gotten her name. "Let's get in the house. It's freezing out here!"

Somehow I got stuck hauling the luggage. It all matched and it was brand new, as if they'd bought it for this trip. It was true they didn't travel much, mostly because of the dog, but they'd brought enough suitcases to last at least a month, and I began to get antsy.

"When is your return reservation for?" I asked Helen. "Just so I can take you to the airport myself."

"Oh, we didn't make one," she answered brightly. "We thought we'd just play it by ear." She took the key out of my hand and unlocked the front door with no trouble whatsoever. I had completely forgotten about Lester. I tried to get in front of Helen, in case he decided to attack, but he just stood there dumbly, looking at me.

"There's our dog," I said nervously, but Helen just went right up to Lester and scratched him behind his droopy ears. "*Him's a good doggy, isn't him?*" she cooed in a baby voice. Lester's tail began to wag so hard that he knocked over the lamp on the end table. There must have been something about Helen that reminded him of Bree. Unfortunately, Lester took an entirely different view of Waffles. The minute Felton stepped through the door, Lester started to bristle. Felton felt Waffles stiffen in his arms and he suddenly sensed a situation.

"*Uh-oh...*" he said.

"Now just stay still, Felton," I started to say, but before I could make a move, Waffles had leapt from his arms and was skittering across the hardwood floor, trying desperately to make it behind the piano. Lester was startled into paralysis for a moment, just long enough for Waffles to wedge himself between the piano and the plaster wall. Then the bigger dog lunged for the smaller one, howling furiously, and he actually managed to nudge the piano half-an-inch. I tried to pull Lester away but it was like trying to move a tank.

Waffles didn't seem particularly frightened, but he wasn't about to leave his sanctuary. Helen ignored the entire fracas. "They just need some time to get used to one another..." she said cheerfully. Hugo nodded, his big silver head bobbing like a giant apple. Felton, realizing that everything was hunky-dory, grinned again and sat down next to Helen as if she were *his* mother instead of Bree's. I'd never seen him behave like this. There was something scary about it.

Hugo slapped me on the back, nearly dislocating my shoulder. "Have a seat, son! Got any gin?"

Lester growled as Waffles scratched an ear. "Now Daddy, you know you shouldn't drink before dinner," Helen said, reaching for her purse. "How about some nice soda instead? I'm sure Brendalee has some Cokes in the ice box."

I cleared my throat. "Brendalee doesn't believe in Cokes."

Felton frowned. "Who's Brendalee?"

I put their bags in our bedroom, since we don't have a guest room, knowing Bree and I would be stuck sleeping on our sofa bed. When we were first married we slept on it in my studio apartment, but somehow we'd managed to wreck the springs, either through our moving it too often or by making love on it too vigorously, and now it was barely preferable to sleeping on the floor. Not that Bree cared. When she's ready to sleep, she sleeps, regardless. But I like a mattress free from protruding wires. We definitely needed a bigger house.

In the living room I could hear of Lester whining at Waffles and Helen chattering, no doubt filling Felton's ear with riveting tales of Bree's early childhood years.

I picked up the phone and called Janie.

"She's not here, Rick. She left hours ago. I think she said something about going to check up on some man she's writing an article about, Bacon, Baymont--"

"Bakersfield??"

"Yeah, that's right!"

I hung up, stunned. I really didn't expect her to pursue this article thing, knowing how I felt about it. Then it occurred to me that maybe she *didn't* know how I felt about it. I'd never said so in so many words, and Bree's not terrific at sensing other people's emotions. Maybe if I just *told* her--

But the more I thought about it the angrier I got. It was humiliating enough to have the man I was supposed to be tailing commit suicide, but now my wife was traipsing around town digging it all up, dragging my two-year-old child with her! I started to work up to a good fury. I'd give her hell when she got home this time! Then I remembered the crew in the living room and realized that it was much more likely going to be the other way around.

By the time I'd returned, Helen had poured iced tea for the whole bunch, and Lester was reluctantly holding still while Waffles sniffed his hindquarters.

"See?" Helen beamed. "I told you they'd get along if we just waited!"

I heard Bree's key in the front lock and started praying.

She backed in, carrying a sleeping Margaret in her arms and hauling two teddy bears, the silky, and her notebook. The dogs went wild.

She spun around and just had time enough to catch my eye, her look murderous, before Helen and Hugo shouted "*Surprise!*"

LIE LIKE A WOMAN

CHAPTER TEN

In the middle of the night the phone rang.

I was lying in the living room on the sofa bed, trying to sleep. This was next to impossible, since every time I turned over a loose spring stuck me right in my sacroiliac. Bree snored softly beside me, wearing my light blue pajamas. I'd never seen her sleep in anything before, and the contrast of her small bones and my oversized nylon pajamas made her unbelievably sexy to me. I suppose she thought if she slept in the nude her parents might get the mistaken impression that we were going to have sex, and Bree made it undeniably clear that as long as they were in the house, *that* wasn't going to happen. Knowing I couldn't have her made me want her even more. Sometimes, if I could arouse her before she was quite awake, she'd forget she was sleeping or sick or unprepared and just go with the flow, so to speak. She wasn't prepared now but it seemed to me it was time we started working on our second child anyway, if we planned to have a second child. After all, neither of us was getting any younger.

Her back was to me and I began to kiss the nape of her neck. I had to lift her hair to do this and she fussed a bit in her sleep. Then I felt her relax and she began to make little noises in her throat. I rubbed her shoulders and bit her ear.

"I'm mad at you," she murmured sleepily.

"You're never mad," I said, not stopping.

"I am now..." she whispered, but she turned toward me anyway. I could smell the fragrance of sleep in her hair as I kissed her. She looked into my eyes and smiled and I knew that no matter how difficult the day had been, in bed we could always communicate. I don't mean just physically, either; I mean that we always let our guard down with each other when we touch, in every way. I took her in my arms--and the phone rang.

I grabbed it up immediately, afraid the house would erupt in a cacophony of babies crying and dogs barking, but no one else woke up. "Who is it?" Bree whispered.

"Who is it?" I said into the receiver.

A small nasal voice came over the earpiece. I couldn't tell if it were male or female.

"*He's got us locked up. He's keepin' us prisoner.*"

"What?"

"*But we know what happened to the other one--*"

"Who is this? What other one?"

"*He didn't jump. He was already dead! We saw him die! That's why he's got us locked up!*"

"Saw *who* die?"

"*Perry Sinker, you nimrod!*"

I heard the receiver click and realized I'd been hung up on. I turned to Bree, dumbfounded.

"Someone says Perry Sinker was dead before he went off the bridge."

She shook her head. "Impossible. Felton was right there every second."

I frowned. "Yeah, you're right. Probably just a crank call. Some kid..." Now that I thought about it, it *did* sound like some kid's voice, although there'd been an urgency to it. Of course, any kid calling at three o'clock in the morning was probably urgently trying not to get caught by his parents. Still...

"He said someone had him locked up...no, that's not right...he kept saying 'we'. '*We saw him die.*'"

"Maybe a witness to the suicide? You think?"

"I don't know *what* to think. Let's forget it." I reached for her again. "I've got better things to think about anyway..."

She pulled away gently. "My diaphram's in our bathroom and I can't get to it without waking up my parents..."

"Let's skinny dip!"

"Sorry," she said firmly. "I'm not ready for another Margaret yet, I've got my hands full as it is." She was fully awake now and not about to take any chances. She kissed me lightly on the cheek and turned over. In a moment she was asleep.

I sighed, squirming as the spring attacked my spine.

This wasn't my case anymore, why was someone calling me at 3 am?

In her sleep Bree murmured "Call Charlie...maybe he can help..."

I grimaced, but she was right. He probably could at that...

CHAPTER ELEVEN

"It was the funniest thing you've ever seen!" Charlie was saying. "Me and Bree sitting in the middle of the floor in the baby's room, searching through a pile of Legos!"

"I'm sorry I missed that," I muttered.

"You should have seen the way Maggie looked at us! I think she was furious that we'd messed up her toys! And she's only two!" He laughed until tears ran down his ruddy cheeks at the memory. I smiled grudgingly. I didn't like the picture of him crawling around on the floor with my wife for any reason.

"I guess she didn't take it after all," he continued, after he'd composed himself. "We never did find it. And what would a two-year-old want with a finger bone anyway?"

"Was that the only part of the skeleton that was missing?" I asked, trying to get back to the subject.

"Yup. Other than that it was a perfectly intact skeleton of a male human, twenty-five to thirty-five years of age."

"Can't you match dental records to identify it?"

Charlie leaned back in his chair expansively. We were sitting in his office, which was infinitely more comfortable than mine, and he was clenching that stupid unlit pipe between his teeth, as usual.

"You know it's impossible to match a dental record unless we have an idea of whose dental record to match. And frankly, right now I'm stumped. I suppose we could just go through all the missing persons reports for the last six months and--"

"Six months? Are you kidding? There wasn't an ounce of flesh left on that thing!"

"Chemically removed. That way you don't have to put up with the stench while the body deteriorates." I made a face. Charlie smiled at my squeamishness. He had never been squeamish; I'd seen him eat a ham sandwich in the autopsy room without missing a bite.

He stood up and started putting on his coat. "Let's go downtown for lunch. I know a great little dive right around the corner from the courthouse where we can get tacos and a beer..."

"The courthouse?"

Charlie smiled wryly, the intelligence in his eyes suddenly biting through that good old boy exterior.

"You want to see your buddy Felton testify this afternoon, don't you?"

* * *

We were late already when we got to the courthouse, and Mel Farley insisted on telling Charlie a joke about a pit bull. It was one of Mel's better efforts, and Charlie was the perfect audience. He was still laughing his booming laugh when I dragged him into the courtroom. Tracy, hearing him, looked up from her table, vast annoyance written all over her face. She was startled to see me, but that was nothing compared to her shock at seeing Charlie. Charlie, on the other hand, looked as if there was no one he would rather see than Tracy.

He took her hand and held it gently. "Tracy, how are you?"

She hesitated for a moment, then managed to sputter, "Charles. What are you doing here?

"Hoping to catch sight of you," Charlie said, smiling sweetly and managing somehow to look both harmless and appealing. Tracy stared at him disbelievingly.

"Me--?" she started, but he instantly scooted around to her side of the table and moved in closer.

"I can't believe how beautiful you look!" he exclaimed in a low whisper, just loud enough for me to hear. "How long's it been?"

Tracy was caught completely off-guard. "I--I don't know..."

"Six years, at least! That's entirely too long. I hear you got married."

"Well, yes--"

"That's a shame," said Charlie. He shook his head sadly. "I have the worst luck..."

"What--?"

"I'm still working for the SDPD. Maybe we could have lunch sometime?"

Tracy opened her mouth, flustered, but before she could refuse him, Charlie pressed his card into her hand.

"I won't take no for an answer, Tracy. You know how persistent I can be..."

He kissed her hand and backed away, his eyes locked to hers. She was hypnotized. Finally he turned and walked me to a seat in the observers' section. I frowned at him.

"What was *that* all about?"

"Just wanted to give Felton a fighting chance. Tracy's petitioned to question him today."

"How do you know that?"

"I'm smarter than I look." Judge Ratchett entered and we all stood. There were only five observers--after all, it wasn't a trial, just an inquest, and supposedly an inquest into a suicide, not the most entertaining of courtroom dramas. There's a lot of tragedy in suicides but usually not a lot of mystery. Most suicides send out warning signals, and a lot of them try it several times before they succeed. So far no one had come up with a motive for Perry's suicide or a body to prove it, but you don't necessarily have to have that, if you had an eyewitness and a reasonable belief that the victim was really dead. That's what Felton was here for.

I looked around. *Where was Felton?*

Charlie realized Felton wasn't there at the same time I did and we craned our necks around toward the door. When a summons says two o'clock in Herman Ratchett's courtroom, you'd better be there at two o'clock or expect to spend the night in jail for contempt.

Tracy, who had been sneaking glances at Charlie, suddenly realized where we were looking and why. She too started staring at the door. Judge Ratchett finished fiddling with the notes on his desk and looked up to see his whole courtroom staring at the swinging doors in the back. His face puckered with irritation. "What the hell--?" he started. The doors suddenly swung open.

In walked Felton, drunk as a skunk.

He wasn't staggering. He was walking very carefully, like a man who could fall off a tightrope at any moment. His hands were unsteady but he was trying very hard to appear dignified. He had cleaned up for the occasion, putting on his very best suit, but he'd lost so much weight that it hung on him unflatteringly, making him appear even shrimpier than he really was. For the first time since I'd known him, his potbelly had disappeared. I caught his eye as he passed. He was scared to death.

Judge Ratchett watched with growing impatience as Felton mounted the witness stand. "I hope you didn't drive to this inquest in that condition, young man," he said.

Felton looked up at him respectfully. "Oh no sir, I didn't. I drove here first and then got drunk in the parking lot."

The judge frowned. "You must have gotten here awfully early."

Felton shook his head solemnly. "No sir. It doesn't take much to make me drunk, 'specially on an empty stomach..."

"You haven't eaten today?"

"Or yesterday either."

"Are you without funds?"

"No...just didn't feel much like eating..."

Judge Ratchett looked alarmed. The idea of Felton not eating for two days must have been appalling to him; he was the Orson Welles of the 6th District. He motioned Simon Wischerath up to the bench.

"Is this the witness to the suicide?"

Simon shuddered. He knew he was not a favorite of this particular judge. "Yes, your honor."

The judge lowered his voice. "Has this witness had a psychiatric evaluation?"

Simon, who had known Felton in the pre-Perry days, looked confused. "Who, Felton?"

Felton, who'd been daydreaming, looked up at the mention of his name. "Huh?"

Judge Ratchett grimaced. "I want this man held for evaluation before he testifies, Mr. Wischerath. *Comprende?*" He turned toward Felton and looked at him almost kindly. "Mr. Shapiro? You may step down." Felton looked up in confusion. He had braced himself for the onslaught and there was no onslaught forthcoming.

"Huh?"

"Mr. Shapiro, I have my doubts about your competency as a witness. I want you held for psychiatric evaluation. Mr. Wischerath will set up an appointment for you with the court psychiatrist. In the meantime, you'll stay with a court-appointed guardian. Understand?"

"Huh?"

Judge Ratchett turned to Simon again. "Find this man a guardian if you have to take him home yourself!"

I found my voice and rose to my feet. "I volunteer, your Honor." I could see Felton deteriorating before my very eyes and I figured I could put him up with Dad if all else failed. I didn't want him staying with strangers. Simon looked hopefully at the judge. He was not anxious to bring Felton home to his wife, a stingy woman who would probably have stuck him in the garage.

Judge Ratchett frowned at me for a moment, then recognized me and nodded his head wearily. "Fine, let Matthews have him. They deserve each other. The rest of you people, out of here."

He stood to go. Tracy, who'd been in a flustered daze since Charlie had spoken to her, suddenly realized that she wasn't going to get the chance to castrate anyone this afternoon.

"Wait a minute! Judge Ratchett!"

He turned to her. "As for you, Mrs. Lowe, I am surprised at you, providing me with a drunken witness!"

"But--"

"You'll have to do better than that if you want to become District Attorney in *this* city! I'm of a mind to cite you with contempt!" He flounced out of the court indignantly.

Tracy was stunned. She stood staring after him, as if flabbergasted by her own bad luck. Then, slowly, she turned until the full blast of her ice- blue eyes landed on me.

"You did this to me!" she hissed. Felton was making his way painstakingly down the aisle, but somehow he missed the fact that Tracy was standing right next to the railing. He swung the gate open sharply and slammed it into Tracy's rump, sending her sprawling onto the polished wooden floor, briefcase and all.

She landed flat on her face. I knew it was funny but I couldn't laugh. Nobody laughed; it was too pathetic. I rushed over to help her up but Charlie reached her first. She looked up at him and I could see to my dismay that there were tears in her eyes.

"Come on, Tracy," Charlie said softly. "I'll take you home..." She didn't object. He got her to her feet, retrieving her briefcase, and they walked gravely from the courtroom. Felton focused on me.

"...*oops*!..." he said.

I realized suddenly that Charlie had driven me here. Luckily Felton had his car, the Bobsled from Hell. I tried to count my blessings.

"Sorry, Rick...can't see to do anything right these days..."

"Forget it, Felton. Someday we'll laugh about this."

"You really think so?"

"Sure. You ever hear the one about the alligator and the two senators?" I kept him moving. I didn't want to hear what Bree would say about this...

CHAPTER TWELVE

"Oh my God! *Felton!*" Rita was out of her seat and at his side in a split second. She turned to me angrily. "What did you *do* to him?"

"I got him drunk," I said sarcastically, amazed at her sudden change of heart. She had always detested Felton, but now she couldn't do enough for him. Before I knew it she had him laid out of the couch in the waiting room and was spoon-feeding him coffee. He seemed almost oblivious. I went into my office and phoned Dad.

"*Hello?*" said a familiar feminine voice.

I knew instantly who it was. "Mom?" Another surprise. As far as I knew, my mother and father hadn't seen each other since my wedding. "What are you doing there?"

"*Rick, darling, can't you say hello like normal people?*" She chuckled that deep throaty chuckle I had always loved as a child and I could almost see the dimples in her cheeks deepening. "*Your poor father is prostrate with pain, and I just came over for a little while to help him out. I think we're going to put him into the hospital this afternoon.*"

"Who's 'we'?"

"*Dr. Clayton and myself, naturally. Looks like his ulcers are acting up again. Dr. Clayton wants to operate.*"

"Dr. Clayton must be ninety-nine years old by now!"

"*He's eighty-two,*" she answered primly, as if that settled the question. My mother has an unerring view of the rightness of things, no doubt where Tracy got it, but with my mother, it is tempered by great beauty and charm, whereas with Tracy, it's simply obnoxious.

"Want me to come over?"

"*I think I can handle it.*" I heard her turn away from the phone and say, "*It's Rick...yes, I'll tell him...*" She turned back and said, "*Your father says to be sure and call Mrs. Zapata.*"

I rolled my eyes. "I will, Mom. How's Jason?"

"*Fine, as always.*" I thought I detected a certain degree of coolness in her answer. Jason has been her husband for ten years. He's a tall handsome tennis player who matched her perfectly; in fact, they look like they were poured out of the same mold. I liked Jason well enough, and I was happy when my mother found him, though it broke Dad's heart. He could never get over the fact that Mom had divorced him, even though he was living with a twenty-seven year old cocktail waitress at the time.

"Mom--"

"*I have to go, darling. I'll keep you informed...*" She hung up and I suddenly realized that I had counted on Dad to store Felton for me--now that was out of the question. I couldn't take him home with me. We already had a full house, although Felton probably would have loved it. He'd taken an inordinate liking to Bree's parents, but I just didn't think we had a spare spot to keep him. Between the dogs and the baby and the in-laws and us, our two-bedroom house was straining at the seams. *Maybe Charlie?...*

I called Charlie's office. He hadn't come back yet from taking Tracy home. I left a message and hung up.

Rita magically appeared at my door. "You've got to do something for Felton," she said, "He's falling apart."

"You got any ideas? I can't even find him a place to stay."

She smiled. "He can stay with me."

"With you? Are you kidding?"

"I have a spare bedroom. No problem."

I smirked. "Yeah, great. How would that look?"

"Rick," she said, fixing me with those black eyes, "I have never in my life given one good solid damn how things look." I had to give her credit: Rita bowed to neither man nor beast. She put on her coat and got Felton upright. "I'll take him home now. He can spend the weekend with me and be fit for human consumption by Monday. You have my number, don't you?"

I frowned. "I don't know. I've never called you at home."

"Bree has it. She calls me all the time." That was news. Felton stood swaying as Rita selected one of Dad's overcoats from the closet and wrapped it around him gently.

"What about his car?" I remembered.

"Have it towed away. We'll get him a new one." Felton heard this and smiled up at Rita gratefully as she inched him out the door.

I sat in the empty office, wondering if I should try to get any work done. My alternative was going home and being forced into a trip to Tijuana on the trolley with Helen and Hugo. It was too cold for that, as far as I was concerned. Unfortunately the only open case I had at the moment involved Delores Zapata and her maniacal twins, who seemed better off lost. But Dad had said to call her. Maybe he knew something I didn't.

It took nearly half an hour for me to figure out how to bring up the phone list on Rita's computer. By this time I was sure that Rita had reprogrammed it specifically to make herself un-expendable, but truthfully I'm no good with computers. They confounded me. I just don't think that way. Bree has a computer at home that she writes her novels on. Before she got it she would write them out longhand and hire a typist to type them for her; now she does everything on the computer. She didn't even have to take lessons. She figured out the whole thing from the manual. She's got a perfect memory, so trial-and-error to her means one error, not twenty in a row like I make. I hate computers, personally. It seems to me we don't have enough to do as it is and that's why so many people get in trouble. Anything defined as a labor-saving device is bad for humanity, in my opinion.

Delores Zapata wasn't home.

"*She's workin' like decent folk*," said her sister, Carmen. "*Don' you work?*" I decided that good manners didn't run in this family and wondered if Carmen were as rotund as Delores.

"Where does she work?" I asked as politely as I could.

"*She does a lot of places, how should I know? On Friday she goes out to La Jolla and cleans that rich lady's house.*" Since there were several thousand rich ladies in La Jolla, I asked her to be more specific. "*I don' remember--*" she answered sullenly, "*--an' why should I tell you? You're the one called me a liar!*"

"Me?"

"*Yeah! You told Delores I never seen her husband with that floozie when I know good and well I did! He's never been no good anyway, kidnappin' those poor little twins like that without a word to no one!*" She hung up on me abruptly and I knew I'd never find Delores at this rate.

Then I remembered that when Delores came here four months ago, Rita had had her fill out a statement of income. Dad had taken one look at Delores and had decided we'd never get paid, but one thing Delores had been absolutely scrupulous about was paying the firm, even though so far we'd had virtually no results. I'm sure she was still hoping.

I started going through Rita's file cabinet. I hadn't looked at it since we'd hired her and I was amazed to find out that she'd set up her own filing system, one that had no relationship to Stack's Manual for Secretaries. For instance, she had the clients filed according, not to their names, but to their personal traits. Some under SWEETIES, some under SOURPUSSES, and some under TIGHTWADS. I found Mrs. Zapata under NICE BUT SCREWY. I suppose Rita got some sort of perverse pleasure out of her classifications, but to me they weren't funny. I pulled out Delores' file and started looking through her references.

Delores had listed several ladies that she'd worked for, none of whom I knew, but one name struck me as familiar, and it only took the synapses a second to put it together. Mrs. Yvonne Cutter.

Marilyn's mother.

The blue-haired widow with the chocolates and the Harlequin romances.

I looked to see how long Delores had been working for Mrs. Cutter. She'd put down: "seven years, give or take". Long enough to have known Marilyn Cutter while she still lived at home. Long enough to have met Carl Bakersfield.

Long enough to have recommended our firm to him, maybe? Because it was a strange coincidence, to say the least.

Suddenly I was very interested in talking to Delores Zapata. After my run-in with Marilyn, I knew the guards were not about to let me onto the estate, but I thought maybe I could wait outside the gates until Delores emerged. Seemed like a good plan.

Then I remembered that Bree had used my Mustang to drop me off at Charlie's that morning and the only car available for me to drive was the Bobsled from Hell. Not exactly inconspicuous, but I'd make do. It was almost quitting time and I didn't want to have to tussle with Carmen again, so I took off. The city dump would just have to wait.

LIE LIKE A WOMAN

CHAPTER THIRTEEN

Delores was just passing through the gates of the mansion on her way to her bus stop when I pulled up to the curb. I was judicious enough to park down the block from the mansion, but I was close enough to hear her saying goodnight to the gorilla at the gate. She came roiling down the sidewalk toward me, no doubt headed toward the bus stop, her three-hundred pounds advancing in even, graceful waves. She was carrying an umbrella but she wasn't wearing an overcoat, although by now it was cold enough to see your breath.

As she passed me I leaned out the window and shouted: "Delores?"

Without even looking at my face she turned viciously and attacked me with her umbrella. I guess the car tipped her off that I was a masher up to no good.

"I'm a married woman, you bastard! You don't talk to me in the street like I'm a whore!" She hit me a couple of times and stopped to take a breath.

"It's Richard Matthews, Delores! Don't hit me again!" I had my hands over my head just in case, and it took her a moment to place me. Then she looked at me in wonder.

"You find my boys?" she whispered hopefully.

"No. I'm sorry," I said, and seeing the way her eyes had shone for a moment, I really was. Appearances to the contrary, I guess a mother just can't help loving her sons. "But I need to talk to you about something else. Here, why don't I give you a ride home?"

I got out and ran around to the other side to open the door for her, which wasn't easy considering that there was no outside handle. Delores waited until I had opened it, just like any lady would, then she wedged herself into the front seat. She eyed the worn cushions for a moment and said, as I pulled away, "You know, I thought you were just another slick city boy. I'm glad to see you don't waste my money on no fancy car."

There was approval in her voice for the first time since she'd met me and I wasn't about to inform her that the car was not mine. We drove down Pacific Coast Highway for a while at a relatively fast clip. Delores seemed to enjoy it, even though the Chevy was rife with drafts and I was freezing to death. She rolled down her window and stuck her head out and jeered at all the people standing at bus stops, nodding her head with satisfaction.

"Someday I'm gonna have me a car just like this!" she said seriously.

"Mrs. Zapata, do you know Carl Bakersfield?"

She frowned. "You mean that creep married to Miz Cutter's daughter?"

"In a manner of speaking."

"I know him," she said shortly. "Don't like him."

"Why not?"

She was looking at herself in the rearview mirror, which hung askew from the front window. She made a face. "Once I took the twins to work with me, ya know? And that Mr. Bakersfield, he got mad at them 'cause they was spying on him and his boyfriend and he locked them in the bathroom. Was they mad! They screamed so loud the misses had to come down and let them out and told them they couldn't come back, no way. But I brought 'em back sometimes anyway, that place is so big no one was the wiser."

"Mrs. Cutter's place?"

"Mr. *Bakersfield's* place! Miz Cutter sent me over there to clean up after Marilyn married him, said she thought he couldn't get good help. That was the truth! He has an evil temper, folks kept up and quitting on him. I finally quit myself right after the boys disappeared. Couldn't stand all the fighting and carrying on and bickering..."

"Between him and Marilyn?"

"Between Marilyn and that so-called secretary of his, that boyfriend! They was always screaming at one another. Dirty language, too. I don't abide by that."

I paused. "Did you ever hear Marilyn and Mr. Bakersfield fight?"

She thought about it a moment. "No," she said finally, "No, can't say as I did. They was always real lovey-dovey, leastways where I could see 'em. But that Perry guy, he slunk around there like a whipped dog! You could tell he wasn't too happy with the situation."

We eased up onto the freeway. Delores lived in East San Diego, a few miles and several light-years away from my neighborhood. I began to realize that this poor woman had sunk all her hard-earned cash into finding her lost children, and now I was grilling her about a case that didn't even belong to me anymore. She didn't own a car, she didn't even have the money to buy a winter coat. The more I thought about it, the worse I felt.

"I've decided to refund your fee, Mrs. Zapata."

She looked at me in anguish for a moment, then opened her mouth and screamed as loud as she could. I swerved and almost hit a jogger.

"They're dead!" she cried. "I knew it! I knew it all along!"

"No, they're not!" I interjected, trying to staunch the flow of tears. Obviously she'd misunderstood me. "Believe me, Mrs. Zapata, your boys are *not* dead!" She calmed down a bit, but her look was skeptical. "I...I just feel the firm hasn't been able to do much for you, and it would be unfair to charge you--"

Her face was wreathed in relief. "Oh, that! It's okay. I know you'll find them!" As abruptly as it came, her anguish passed and she started looking out the window again. We stopped for a light.

Abruptly we were hit from behind. Hard.

I looked back at the offending car, a black 1987 Pontiac. I gritted my teeth, knowing that the driver had to be one of the vast uninsured that California law is supposed to protect me from, and I started resignedly to get out of the car to call the police. But before I could get the door open, the Pontiac backed up a few feet, then sped forward and rammed the back of Felton's car again.

Delores looked around in disgust. Disgust turned to shock. "That's Fred! That's my *husband!*"

"Your husband? Now what the hell--" Delores' husband had been missing since the twins disappeared. In fact, she was convinced that he was the one that had taken them.

Fred backed up his Pontiac and aimed it at our rear.

"Fred!" Delores shrieked joyfully. "Where you been, Honeylamb?"

"Son of a bitch!" shouted Fred, his face a mask of fury. "I'll teach you to fool around with my wife!" He charged once again. This time I heard the crunch of metal. The light changed. I decided some distance between us might be a good idea and I floored the pedal.

Delores turned to me angrily. "What are you driving away for? I keep telling you, that's Fred!"

I tried to catch a glimpse of him in the rearview mirror. He looked furious.

"Sorry, Delores, but I think that your hubby there suspects that you and I--"

She looked at me uncomprehending for a moment, then wrinkled up in disgust. "Why that cheap, dirty minded little--"

I slammed on the brakes as we hit another red light. Behind me Fred slammed on his brakes, too late. His car hit Felton's again, this time locking bumpers. He tried to back away, but he succeeding only in wearing the rubber off of his already-bald tires. He jumped out of the Pontiac and slammed the door as hard as he could.

"Son of a bitch! I hate this son of a bitchin' car!"

He kicked the fender viciously. It fell off. Delores watched calmly as Fred vented his fury on the car. Finally he sat down hard on the asphalt as the vehicles behind us swerved around him, and the drivers leaned out of their windows and hurled Spanish curses at him.

Fred put his head in his hands and sobbed. Delores managed to kick open her door. She went over to Fred and knelt down beside him.

"Serves you right! Thinkin' I would cheat on you. I'm a God-fearing woman!"

He looked up at her and she smiled radiantly. I was trying to separate the bumpers but they didn't seem to notice. Fred looked around. "Where's the twins?" he asked.

"I thought you stole them," said Delores. "I guess they really was kidnapped." She patted him on the head. "Either that or they run away." She jerked a thumb in my direction. "I hired this guy to find them, though he ain't done such a hot job so far."

I stood up on top of Felton's back bumper and bounced until the cars parted company. I'd had about enough of this reunion.

Fred eyed me suspicious. "You some sort of private dick?"

"Yeah."

"Then I guess I won't clobber you. I was going to, but now there don't seem to be no point."

I agreed.

"You gonna find our boys?" he asked hopefully.

"I'm trying," I said.

"Try harder," he answered sternly. He seemed to have composed himself. He took Delores by the arm and steered her toward the Pontiac. I got into the Bobsled and started the engine.

As I drove away I heard Delores say, "Was you with a blonde floozy in a bowling alley last week, by any chance?"

I didn't stick around for his answer.

CHAPTER FOURTEEN

When I got home, Bree was sitting sullenly at the table in our kitchen while her mother broiled steaks in the oven. The odor of singed meat was wonderful--around our house we seldom get meat, because of Bree's concerns for our health, and sometimes I really miss it. Obviously Bree didn't. She looked at me and rolled her eyes in frustration as Helen chattered away happily.

"Your sister Audrey's boys are so well-behaved and Audrey gives them all the candy they want! I don't know why you won't give your little baby just a few M & M's--"

"I don't like for her to have candy, Mother. It makes her hyper."

"That's just a myth! You grew up on chocolate bars!"

"I was a *maniac*. I practically got thrown out of kindergarten because I couldn't sit still!"

"You were just bored--you were such a *smart* little thing. Always with your nose in some book, I could never get you to go outside with the other kids. That's probably why you turned out so small..."

"I probably turned out so small because my growth was stunted by all that chocolate!" Bree said, bristling. "It's a miracle my brain wasn't stunted, too!"

Helen looked at Bree innocently. "I don't know what you're so upset about. Of course, you always were high strung..."

Bree looked at me helplessly. I shrugged. Every time Bree got together with her mother for any length of time, she became a different woman. The two of them bickered like that constantly. I told Bree to just ignore Helen, but she couldn't somehow. She lit on her every phrase with a paranoid delight, choking all the hidden meaning from it.

"I don't know how you cook in this kitchen," Helen continued blithely. "You don't have the proper utensils, Brendalee; Daddy always says, the right tools for the right job! Why don't we go down to K-Mart and buy you some decent knives? Don't worry, I'll pay for them, I know how you worry about money."

"I don't worry about money, Mother. I make plenty of money."

Helen smiled sympathetically. "Of course you do, dear. But this is a very expensive city to live in. If you were back in Kansas City--"

Bree began to flush. I wisely decided to see what the boys in the back room were having.

Hugo was sitting at Bree's desk, playing with her computer. He fancied himself somewhat of an expert in electronics, even though before he retired he had owned a shoe store.

"Might buy myself one of these babies," he boomed when he saw me, fiddling with the keys. "Was it hard to learn how to use it?"

"I don't know," I said "I never *have* learned how to use it." He fiddled with the keys some more and managed to bring up some sort of list on the screen.

"See? Simple!" he beamed. "Why, I'd get the hang of this in no time!"

I glanced over his shoulder casually. The list seemed to consist of chores Bree had appropriated for different days this week. Bree loved to make lists. She made them for groceries, for cleaning, for writing--she'd even made a list the day before we were married headed "WEDDING". I had the feeling she'd made this particular list before her parents had surprised her with their visit--otherwise it wouldn't have been so long and complicated. I ran down it quickly, guiltily, but there was nothing unusual.

Confirm babysitter for Friday, Check on car, Pick up keys to warehouse...

Pick up keys to warehouse? I must have read that wrong. I glanced back just as Hugo managed to erase the screen.

"Damn!" he said brusquely. "Not as easy as it looks!" He turned to me and grinned. He was a handsome Irishman who liked his liquor, and his freckled red face was all curling lines. Actually, Margaret looks a lot like him in her own baby way, and she could do worse. I liked Hugo almost as much as I liked my own father. He was impossible not to like.

"Can you bring up that list again? I want to check something..." I said, trying to sound casual. Hugo screwed up his mouth and concentrated, pressing this key and that. Sweat broke out on his forehead. I'd seen him mow his acre of lawn on a muggy summer's day without even perspiring, but this effort seemed to take a lot out of him. Finally a list appeared on the screen.

It was labeled: "BABY CLOTHES".

I smiled weakly at Hugo. "Well, you tried," I said. Hugo looked defeated. I watched him rummage around in Bree's desk drawers, feeling somewhat violated. Hugo managed to find the computer manual he was looking for, along with several unidentified notebooks, which I guessed were handwritten manuscripts of her earlier novels. He slammed shut the drawer triumphantly and opened the book to the first page. "Now we'll see who's smarter than a damned machine!" he shouted. "I'll know this thing inside and out before I'm through!" He grinned up at me. "All it takes is a little tenacity, son! That's what I always told my kids! All it takes is a little tenacity!"

* * *

I awoke that night to find Bree standing beside the fold-out couch, climbing into on a pair of black stretch leggings. She was already wearing her black turtleneck and as I watched, she pulled on her black sneakers.

"Just where do you think you're going?" I said, startling her. "You look like a cat burglar."

95

"I *am* a cat burglar, and there happens to be a particularly lovely cat down the street that I have to burgle."

I smiled. "Why don't you stay home and burgle me instead?" She smiled back and pulled a flashlight out of her purse. I began to get alarmed.

"Bree?"

"I'll be back before you know it..." she whispered, starting for the door.

"Hold it!"

"*Shhhh*, you'll wake the baby!"

"I'm coming with you!"

She frowned. "You won't like it..."

"Try me," I said.

* * *

"I *hate* this," I said.

It was freezing. I was wearing black jeans and my black turtleneck, when what would have been far more appropriate was a heavy wool parka. It's usually cooler down by the water anyway, but this was ridiculous. For all the luck with weather we were having, we might as well have packed it in and moved back to the Midwest. At least Helen would be happy.

We had parked the Mustang five blocks away and Bree had insisted on going down back alleys to get here. As nearly as I could figure we were somewhere in the warehouse district directly beneath the bridge. It was chilly and foggy and the fish smell was nauseating. My bones ached and my muscles were stiff with cold. I wanted to go home.

"Do you have the key?" I mumbled.

"Rita couldn't get it for me," Bree whispered back.

"What does Rita have to do with this?" I asked, irritated.

"Nothing. But she knows people...she's been helping me..." She leaned down and tried to look through the keyhole of the large bay doors in front of us. The warehouse seemed smaller than the ones surrounding us, and it had obviously seen better days. There was no sign on it, though I could vaguely make out ghostly letters of one that had recently been painted over.

"Why doesn't she ever help *me*?" I growled.

"Why don't you ever ask her?" Bree said. I didn't have an answer for that one. Bree looked up at the windows above us.

"Maybe they're not locked..."

"Maybe it'll snow in Malibu..."

She smiled sweetly. "Don't say that. They're predicting snow in Malibu."

I shivered. "I believe it..." The fog had subsided sometime while I slept and now a full moon hung ripe over the bay. If it hadn't been so cold and I hadn't been so sleepy, I could actually have appreciated it, but it was and I was so I said: "Is it absolutely necessary that we break into this building tonight?"

"Yes," said Bree, not mincing words. "It is."

I looked up. There was a rickety fire escape that led to the third story and then the roof. I sighed. "Let's go."

I jumped as high as I could, suddenly aware of the extra ten pounds I had carried since Bree's pregnancy, and snared the fire escape. It pulled down creakily and we started climbing, trying to be as inconspicuous as possible considering that the thing probably hadn't been used in ten years and it made a racket like a sinking ship.

"Pull it back up," Bree whispered, "that way no one will follow us."

"Who's going to follow us at this time of night? Who in his right mind would be out here in the freezing cold at this time of night?"

"*Shhhh!*"

I'm always amazed that someone as small and delicate-looking as Bree can be so athletic--she climbed smoothly and agilely, swinging over the rail on the second floor to try the window.

It was locked.

"Let's go on up," she said, pointing to the third floor. The window there had a large crack right down the middle of it. "Maybe we can push the glass out without making too much noise." She started up the stairs. I grabbed at her jacket.

"Did it occur to you that what you're about to attempt is patently illegal?"

Bree looked at me as if the thought had never entered her head. "It's research."

"For what?"

"For my article. For my book."

"Tell that to the judge."

She smiled at me affectionately and pulled my earlobe. "Richard, you worry too much." She was just leaning down to kiss me, something she is wont to do when she thinks nobody is watching, when we heard the car engine.

Below us a patrol car was pulling up into the parking lot directly beneath the fire escape.

"Now who would be out patrolling the neighborhood at this time of night?" Bree started indignantly, but I went "*Shhhhh!*" and pushed her against the rough bricks. The patrol car stopped and its headlights blinked off abruptly. We waited for a moment, half-expecting a bevy of bluecoats to jump out, revolvers drawn, but nothing happened. No one got out. Nothing moved.

After five minutes, we slowly eased away from the wall and moved up the fire escape, keeping one eye on the patrol car at all times. Still nothing happened. Bree reached the window and leaned over to try to open it. She miscalculated and accidentally nudged the broken pane; the bottom half loosened and dropped from the frame, but amazingly it fell on a large piece of canvas and didn't break. Bree looked at me gleefully, then turned and eased herself into the open part.

"Watch out," I hissed, "You'll cut yourself!" But before I could stop her she had disappeared into the dark interior. I waited for a moment, shivering with the cold; then the latch clicked and Bree opened the door slowly. I looked down at the patrol car. Still nothing. I stepped inside, not knowing what to expect.

Bree shoved a flashlight into my hands and pointed toward the right. "Go that way", she said, still whispering. "I'll see what's by the staircase."

"What am I looking for?"

"I don't know."

I shrugged. "That should be easy to find." I tried to turn on the flashlight. Nothing happened. No doubt the battery was dead.

I jiggled it a couple of times, and the light came on, faintly, then faded. I found if I held the flashlight with both hands and kept up a continuous jiggling motion, the light would stay on. I felt like a fool, but Bree had already disappeared around a corner with *her* flashlight. It was too late to trade.

The warehouse was cluttered in places and empty in others, but the things it was cluttered with didn't make any sense. There seemed to be canvas covering virtually everything, and there was a thick layer of dust on the canvas. There was also a thick layer of dust on the floor, which indicated to me, at least, that no one had been here for some time. I don't know what it indicated to Bree. I couldn't find her.

"*Bree*?" I said in a stage whisper. There was no answer. I was furious, but it was just like Bree not to have any regard for my feelings. I worried about her constantly anyway, since she seemed to have absolutely no concept of the word danger, which on the outside of it seems admirable, but the truth was, she was always putting herself in jeopardy and I was always having to cope with it. Her answer to that was that nothing had ever happened to her so far so why should she worry? Great. It was the "so far" that bothered me.

The canvasses made great hulking shadows as my light played over them, lending to the already-spooky atmosphere of the place. I reached out and lifted the cover off one of the heaps. Underneath was a pile of boxes, maybe fifty in all. They were sealed with gray packing tape. I located the one closest to me, and, knowing better, slit the seal with my pocket knife. Inside were books of every kind and variety. Fifty boxes of books. Whoever owned them must be quite a reader.

I picked up a paperback with a lurid cover. The title was *The Killer Within Me* and it had one of those oil painting covers that were so popular in the forties; it was an old book, probably a collector's item. I flipped open the front cover, trying to keep the flashlight jiggling while I juggled the book.

Inside, on the title page, was a small sticker with a drawing by Beardsley and a handwritten inscription that read: "*From the library of Perry Sinker*".

"*Aha*!" cried a voice next to my ear. I jumped a foot, dropping my flashlight.

"You seem a little nervous..." said Bree mildly, "...I see you made a discovery."

I got down on my hands and knees to locate my flashlight, which naturally had rolled under another canvassed pile. "Did you know that Perry Sinker's books were here?"

"No. All I knew was that Carl Bakersfield rented this warehouse about five months ago. I had no idea what he was using it for. No one does, apparently."

I felt something furry slither beneath my fingers, but I wasn't about to say anything. My flashlight was out of reach, so I stood up, mustering my last shred of my dignity.

"What else did you find?"

"Nothing so far. Haven't looked." I reached over and took her flashlight rather brusquely. "We'll have to share." At least she couldn't wander off from me now.

Together we started searching the piles. It seemed that everything that Perry Sinker had ever owned was in this room: furniture, books, mementoes, even high school yearbooks.

"Maybe now that he's dead, Carl just couldn't bear to have his things around."

I shook my head. "No one's been up here for months. He must have stored them long before Perry died." I couldn't say that I blamed him. The furniture was of a particularly noxious fifties pseudo-sophisticated style, with a lot of angles and too much aqua upholstery. Speckled ashtrays with cigarette burns, skinny lamps, a kidney-shaped coffee table with a boomerang motif. I hated that stuff.

The books, though, seemed to fascinate Bree. A lot of them had to do with real-life crime: psychiatric studies, case histories, famous criminals' biographies. There was also an abundance of classic mystery and suspense novels. She smiled. "I wonder if Carl would be willing to sell these..."

"We already have more books than we have bookshelves. Besides, if Carl figures out we've been in his warehouse, you can check them out of the prison library. He's out to get me as it is."

"Well, he's bound to figure out that *someone* has been here. You left a calling card." She pointed to the floor, where the light from my wayward flashlight skidded across the dust. The thing wouldn't stay on when I was holding it, but it seemed to have gotten its second wind. "Not to mention the footprints."

"I won't mention them. Let's get out of here." I eased out through the door onto the fire escape. The patrol car was still below us, but there were no signs of life.

"How are we going to get past *that?*" I said to Bree.

She looked down. The patrol car was right beneath the fire escape. I looked at her hopefully. "Maybe there's another exit?"

She shook her head. "I checked. They're all padlocked. We'll just have to climb over it."

"Climb over it? Are you *nuts?* Never mind. Stupid question..." She ignored me and started down the fire escape. It was true that we hadn't seen a sign of life--maybe whoever was in the patrol car was asleep. At any rate, we didn't seem to have any choice.

We got to the first level without incident; then I miscalculated and lowered the bottom stairs as slowly and quietly as I could. Unfortunately the rope slipped from my hand and the ladder swung down and crashed right into the front fender of the police car.

The sound of the crash rang through the silent night and suddenly the passenger side door sprang open. "Jump!" I yelled at Bree. It was only about eight feet down and I figured if we didn't break our legs we could make a run for it. Bree hopped nimbly down on top of the police car; then, for good measure, jumped up and down a few times, trying to perplex the occupant, no doubt. I could see that she wasn't a bit afraid--in fact, she was getting a tremendous kick out of all this. There was a shriek from inside the car and who should come tumbling out the opposite sides but a half-dressed Charlie--and my sister Tracy!

They looked up at us in shock as I shone the flashlight down in Tracy's face. Bree was still jumping up and down gleefully, but she stopped when she saw my expression. She followed my glance and, seeing Charlie in his state of disarray, her face fell with profound disappointment. She climbed down from the car. "Some things never change..." she said, shaking her head.

Somehow Charlie being there did not surprise me; he seemed to be everywhere I was and I felt lucky to get off without a bullet in my back. But Tracy!--I was grinning from ear to ear. Caught in the act!

"Tracy!" I beamed, jumping down easily as she tried to smooth her dress. "Well, well, well!"

"Shut up, Rick!" She spat. "I don't want to hear it!"

"But you're a married woman, Trace," I said in an exaggerated manner. "What if your voting constituency should hear of this? A forty-year-old attorney parked in a warehouse lot like some horny kid? For shame!"

She reached out a high-heeled foot and kicked me in the shin as hard as she could. I yelped and danced around on one leg for a minute. Bree looked utterly disgusted. I was just about to belt Tracy one when Charlie chivalrously stepped in.

"That's enough," he said sternly.

"She kicked me first!" I shouted.

"We're adults now," Charlie said calmly.

"Really?" I sneered. "Then why didn't you take her to your apartment instead of screwing her in your car like a teenage Romeo, *hmmmm*?"

Charlie's face went red and for the first time since I'd met him he was angry. Really angry.

"My apartment's being fumigated, not that it's any of your business! We're overage--"

"That's the truth!"

"--and we know what we're doing! You had no right to follow us here!"

I looked at Bree and she looked at me. I almost laughed. It was just like Charlie to miss the implications of us being here; sometimes I wonder how he ever made detective. Bree frowned a warning at me. She wasn't telling. I kept silent.

Charlie seemed to calm down. "I realize you're only looking out for Tracy's best interests, but this is going a little far, isn't it? After all, she's a grown woman."

All the starch seemed to go out of Tracy and she slumped against the brick wall.

"What made you come here, anyway?" I said. "Wouldn't a drive-in have been more appropriate?"

Charlie caught Bree's eye and tried to smile. She glared at him. He turned away guiltily. "It was just a place Tracy knew-- one of her clients owns this building..."

Tracy looked up, frowning at me, trying to put two and two together. She stared at my outfit suspiciously. "Is that what you usually wear when you're tailing someone?" Then she saw Bree. "And shouldn't you be home looking after your baby? What *is* this, anyway?"

"Now Tracy--"

"You're here on your own, aren't you? This has something to do with Carl!"

"Carl?" Charlie was confused.

"Bakersfield! He's the client that owns this warehouse! These two have been up to something, I can guarantee it!" she shouted triumphantly.

"Look who's talking!" I sneered. She suddenly remembered her situation and backed down a bit.

"What I was doing wasn't illegal..."

"But it was adulterous, wasn't it, Trace? What would the voters say? Not to mention your husband."

She thought about that for a moment, considering.

She looked up at me. "All right. You win. I won't tell if you won't."

I grinned, feeling closer to her than I had in years.

"You're on!"

She almost smiled. But didn't.

* * *

It seemed Bree was still in a state of high dungeon when Charlie and Tracy finally left. She sat on the bottom rung of the fire escape, staring at the bridge. She hadn't said a word in ten minutes and somehow I felt hurt that *she* was hurt. Charlie wasn't her husband anymore, so why should she care who he

103

was involved in illicit affairs with? I was the one who should be upset; after all, it was my sister he was corrupting. But somehow even I had trouble imagining Charlie, or anyone else, for that matter, talking Tracy into doing something she was reluctant to do. She must have been willing. More than willing.

"Bree?"

She didn't answer. She just stared at the bridge.

"Honey, let's go home. I'm tired."

She turned toward me in the moonlight then, her face pale with excitement.

"Come up here, Richard!"

I climbed onto the lower rung, stiff with cold. My watch said five a.m. and in just a few hours I was going to have to be at work--then I remembered. It was Saturday. Halloween.

Bree's birthday.

"Look up there," Bree whispered, pointing at the bridge. I looked.

"I don't see anything."

She scowled, as she always did when she thought I was being dense.

"Up there!" she hissed. "Under the railing."

I squinted into the dark. Then I saw what she was talking about--beneath the railing was a ledge I hadn't noticed before. Big enough to stand on.

"Charlie wouldn't throw away those books if he thought Perry were coming back..."

"Felton saw him jump."

"Where's the body?"

"Eaten by sharks?"

"It would be hard but not impossible. Perry goes over the edge, then catches the ledge and hides there. Maybe he has a change of clothes underneath the ones he's wearing. He bloodies the ones he has on and drops them into the water, then, when all the commotion lets up, climbs back up onto the bridge and thumbs a ride! No body!"

"Why?"

"So we'll think he's dead."

"Why, I repeat."

"I don't know," she said calmly. "But there's a reason. Your midnight caller was right. Maybe you should ask *him* why."

"I don't know who he is."

"Maybe he was Perry Sinker..."

I looked at her warily. Sometimes her mind worked in ways I can only describe as downright bizarre.

"I think you're punchy with exhaustion. Let's go home and sleep late."

"With the TV next to our heads?" she grinned. "Not likely."

We dropped down to the ground and I pushed her in the direction of the car. I'd think about it tomorrow.

LIE LIKE A WOMAN

CHAPTER FIFTEEN

I staggered into the kitchen at six-thirty the next morning, after the blare of "*Th-th-that's all, folks!*" had ripped me unceremoniously from a sound sleep. Helen looked up as I came in. "Where's Brendalee?"

"Still out cold. I don't think she slept much last night..."

She frowned. It was her opinion that anyone who slept past sunrise was sleeping the day away. When she was at home in Kansas she would call us around seven a.m. her time, which was five a.m. our time, and she always feigned surprise that we were still in bed. "I've been up for hours," she'd remark.

"Well, it's her birthday, I guess," Helen said reluctantly. "Let her sleep." I wasn't about to do anything else. Although Bree doesn't sleep much, when she *does* sleep, she wants to *sleep*. Waking her is something you don't want to do unless you're armed.

I looked around for Hugo. "Where's grandpa?" I asked Margaret, who was deeply involved with a freshly-baked blueberry muffin. Helen answered for her.

"He went down the street to find a morning paper. I just don't understand how you two can live without a daily paper! Don't you want to know what's going on in the world?" Helen put a plateful of bacon and eggs in front of me. They were as perfect as a picture on a menu.

"We watch CNN," I said between bites.

"Well..." she said, frowning. "That's not the same thing, is it?" She stood with her arms crossed, watching me eat. I don't remember her ever sitting down and eating with the family; she always stands nearby, in case someone needs something. That's probably how she's kept her girlish figure; she's as curvy and slim as Bree, even though she's a good five inches taller.

Margaret looked up from her muffin, her face a study in smudged blueberries. "Twick-or-tweet, Grandma!" she shouted.

Helen beamed. "Trick-or-treat, honey!" she shouted back, giving her a big hug and kiss. Helen was wonderful with Margaret. She had infinite patience and energy and could sit and play with her for hours after Bree and I would have been depleted. I asked Bree if Helen had been that kind of mother to her when she was little and she answered, grudgingly, "Yes. Just the same. She never changes..."

I took another bite of bacon and heard a sound like a strangled whine coming from beneath the table. Before I knew it Waffles was in my lap and helping himself to my bacon. Margaret looked up and started giggling. "Bad Waffles," she gurgled. Helen noticed and came over to me. She snatched Waffles off my lap and sat him down on the floor in front of his dog bowl, which she filled with the remainder of the bacon. No wonder he was so fat. "He just loves his bacon, don't you, Big Boy?" Waffles snorted in satisfaction, but somehow the bacon had suddenly lost its appeal for me. I pushed away from the table. "Maybe I'll just go check on Bree's garden..." Margaret and Helen ignored me, entranced with the sight of the dachshund making a pig of himself. I wandered through the double doors into the backyard.

At least the sun was shining for a change, and it was cool instead of cold, but nothing near the eighty degree weather I was used to for this time of year. Bree's garden had suffered during this cold snap. Nothing had died, really; the plants just looked uncomfortable. Usually her garden runs rampant--vines coiling around stalks, wisps of one plant competing with flowers of another, a haphazard sort of arrangement that imitates nature without insulting it. Bree loved the soil, loved getting firmly into it, digging her hands up to the wrists in that sandy dirt that was the desert before our forefathers decided to landscape. Bree would come in from a day in the yard almost as filthy as Margaret, dirt in her hair, her ears. In all other ways she's fastidious, but she does love to get muddy.

Poor old Lester was sulking near his doghouse. He had decided that Waffles was really the housedog in the family and that he, as a rustic breed, much preferred the open skies. He was obviously jealous, but had the mistaken impression that Waffles was somehow his superior and had to be deferred to. I wondered if we'd ever be able to woo him back into the house. He looked displaced, like Felton. Seeing him so unhappy made me like him a little better, so I went over and patted him. "Good Lester," I said, stroking his head. He licked my hand half-heartedly, which was a definite step forward in our relationship. But he wasn't really up to conversation.

Margaret stuck her blueberry face out to back door. "Daddy! Quick! Quick!" I ran into the kitchen, thinking maybe Helen had had a heart attack or a stroke, at the very least, but there was no body on the floor. Margaret's eyes were dancing. "Mommy's car! Mommy's car!"

We ran through the house to the front door. There with Helen stood a half-asleep, irritated Bree, watching as a man in a striped uniform of some sort pulled into the driveway in a black Mustang Turbo.

Exactly like mine.

"Isn't that nice?" Helen gushed. "Matching cars! That's so cute!"

The man in the uniform parked the car in the driveway and came up to the front door carrying a delivery slip on a clipboard. "B.L. Matthews?" he inquired generally.

"Me!" screamed Margaret, reaching for the clipboard. The man looked at her dubiously. Bree reached out silently and took the clipboard, signing in her precise, tiny hand. The man grinned at her blue pajamas and handed her the keys. "Hot car!" he said enviously. "Enjoy!" He took off running down the street, as if he knew he were late for a bus, but as he reached the middle of the block, a red flatbed truck with white lettering on the side stopped and picked him up.

Bree tried to squeeze past me to the front door, obviously intending to go immediately back to sleep. I stepped in front of her. "You bought a car just like mine?"

She looked at me drowsily. "Yes."

"Used?"

"Just slightly. The original driver drove it home, shut the garage door, turned on the ignition, and committed suicide. It's been in storage ever since."

I was appalled. "Someone died in that car?"

"No, actually, I think he died in the ambulance on the way to the hospital."

Helen barged in. "Well I hope you got a good price on it--no one wants a killer car, after all!"

Bree frowned in Helen's direction. "It's not a killer car, Mother--

"Why would you buy a car exactly like mine?"

Bree looked at me clearly now and I think she finally got the idea that I wasn't too happy. She looked surprised. "Because I *wanted* one just like yours. Besides, I thought it was *ours*, not yours."

"You know what I mean."

"No I don't."

"I just mean that a car should be--unique, you know, it should fit the driver's personality..."

Bree raised an eyebrow. I decided not to pursue this line of thought after all. Anyway, what difference did it make? It was better than a beat-up jeep.

Bree yawned. "I'm going back to bed now." She went into the house and retreated down the hallway as we followed on her heels. She turned to us as she stepped into the bedroom. "Don't anyone say 'happy birthday'," she said.

"Happy birthday!" Helen and I said guiltily, but it was too late. She'd already shut the door.

* * *

"I'm a *witch!*" Margaret boasted. It was five p.m. and almost dark, and Bree was repairing Margaret's witch mask. Margaret had managed to pull the wart off the nose with her teeth, and Bree, who's good at such things, was gluing it back on with some of Helen's fingernail glue. I think Helen would have infinitely preferred for Margaret to be costumed as a fairy princess, or at least a clown, but all year long Margaret had been saying that she wanted to be a witch for Halloween, and Bree's a great believer in taking children's requests seriously. For some reason Margaret had fixated on the Wicked Witch of the West when she saw "The Wizard of Oz" for the first time last spring. I guess the idea of frightening people thrilled her.

Bree and I were going escort Margaret around the neighborhood for her very first Halloween. Helen wanted to come, but she settled instead for a few snapshots at the door with her new automatic digital toy. Margaret refused to take off her mask, which was entirely too big for her, so there was no way of knowing what child lurked behind it, but Helen didn't care. She snapped away anyway with that greedy enthusiasm reserved for grandmothers of small cute children. I felt guilty watching her, knowing that she was a much more entranced grandmother than my own mother was, yet she had very little access to this particular grandchild. It wasn't really my fault--if anything, it was Bree's aversion to the Midwest that kept us on the coast, but I vowed that I'd try harder to see to it that Margaret got the benefit of Bree's parents while she had the chance. My own grandmothers had both died before I was born, and I always felt lacking in unconditional love. It wasn't something you could take for granted, after all. Who else would give it to you besides your grandmother?

It was a freezing night and Margaret's costume was barely visible beneath her overcoat. Bree was wrapped up in black jeans and a fur-lined parka (not real fur; she didn't believe in fur) and her auburn hair was tied up on top of her head in a way I disliked, but tendrils of it blew down in her face and even though she turned thirty-five today, she looked as young and scrubbed as the day I'd met her.

It took Margaret a while to catch onto trick-or-treating. Being a novice, she assumed that when someone opened the door to you, you walked in. The woman next door stood stupidly by as

Margaret walked into her kitchen, and I had to grab her before she helped herself to the lady's apple pie, but after the lady dumped almost her entire store of candy into Margaret's decorated orange bag, she got the idea. Bree was laughing so hard at Margaret's mistake that she almost got run over by a teenager in a Batman costume on a crepe paper-festooned black bike, and an hour later I was carrying Margaret's cache back to the house, and Bree was carrying Margaret, who had run out of energy and fallen asleep.

I thought I recognized some of the cars in front of our house, but it was still a shock when Bree opened the door and a roomful of friends and relatives shouted, "Happy Birthday!"

CHAPTER SIXTEEN

The party was a disaster. Bree's mother Helen had somehow gotten hold of Bree's Roledex, and she'd invited everyone listed in it that she either knew personally or that she'd heard about from Bree. Of course Charlie was there, being the favored ex-husband (Helen thought he walked on water and could never understand why Bree would want to leave him). Bree avoided him, and neither one of us mentioned Tracy, who did not put in an appearance. There was a smattering of Bree's publishing friends from Harcourt-Brace as well as my mother, who had not seen Bree's parents since the wedding, and Rita, with Felton in tow. Felton was the life of the party. He sat in a corner sobbing and refusing to eat, and then took it into his head to search our bathroom for sleeping pills or loose razor blades. Charlie and I had to take the door off the hinges to get him out of there. I wanted to whisk him off to a psychiatric ward, but Rita insisted that I leave him to her, and she took him home. Bree's father got drunk and accidentally stepped on Waffles and broke one of his front legs, and the party ended when Manley Manning, Bree's editor, got into a fight with Bree over some bit of literary trivia and Bree tore up her contract and went to sulk in her new car. Bree had never shown even the slightest hint of temper in all the years I'd known her, but her mother just shook her head smugly, as if it were something she was used to. "That child was always so moody..." she said.

After everyone left I went out to the car and climbed in. Naturally Bree had neglected to lock the doors, even though it was two o'clock in the morning and the street was not well-lit. A couple of teenage ghouls came screaming by on day-glow painted motorcycles, howling at the full moon in not very convincing baritones.

"Bree?"

Silence.

"This is all my fault, isn't it?"

"Yes," came the muffled reply.

"I never should have let them come, should I?"

"No."

"I'm sorry. I kind of got caught in the middle."

She had been leaning her head on the padded steering wheel, but she looked up at me when I said this, her eyes sharp. "Richard, you seem to have a knack for getting caught in the middle. Sometimes I think you cultivate it."

That took me aback.

"What do you mean? Why would I want to do a thing like that?"

"So you won't have to make any decisions. It's much easier to dodge the blame if it looks like you're being forced into things because you're such a nice guy."

"Are we about to have our first fight?"

She thought about that for a moment. "Maybe..." The analytical way she said it made my blood run cold. It could never remember her criticizing me. I was always the one who was finding fault with her, but as far as I knew, she thought I was perfect. She'd never complained about me before, at any rate. It hadn't occurred to me that she might be holding something back.

I steeled myself. "What else, Bree? Maybe you should let it all out."

She stared at me neutrally, then looked out the window. "Let what out?"

"The years of resentment. Go ahead, I can take it," I said, my stomach in a knot.

April Campbell Jones

She looked at me incredulously; then she started to laugh. She was genuinely amused. She saw that I was serious and on the verge of breaking down and my chagrin made her laugh even harder. Tears came into her eyes and she reached for my hand and squeezed it warmly.

"There's no resentment--not for you, anyway. I love you, don't you know that? I'd tell you if something were wrong. You should know me well enough to know that I don't keep things inside."

"Then why have you been acting so weird?"

She rolled her eyes sheepishly. "It's my *mother*. She makes me crazy. I don't know why, it's always been that way. Maybe it's that way with all mothers and daughters. That's a sobering thought. Do you think that in twenty-five years Margaret will be sitting out here with her husband in the freezing cold?"

"In twenty-five years California will be at the bottom of the ocean and we'll be ready for the nursing home." I drew her close to me and she snuggled against my chest. It really was beginning to get cold. I had to remember to touch her the next time we were on the verge of a fight; she was like a cat. "I'm sorry you're having a hard time..."

She sighed. "I hate it when I whine. It's sickening and self-centered and a waste of time..." Under her breath, she said, "*Shut up, Bree.*"

I laughed. "We'd better go in. Isn't that your mother peering out of our front window shutters?"

Bree looked grim. "Just like high school..." she said hotly. She looked at me. "I hate scenes." She got out of the car and went inside. I followed.

* * *

Sundays around our neighborhood are wonderful, if you happen to enjoy the sound of chainsaws and lawnmowers. People who spend the whole week waking to an alarm clock for some reason think that it's absolutely necessary when the weekend comes to knock that dead limb off the oak tree in their backyard just before breakfast, or to make sure the hedges are

115

trimmed before the dew has had time to dry. For me sleep is a sacred thing, but being a family man meant that no matter how late I was up the night before, at seven a.m. promptly something loud would interrupt my dreams and I'd come jolting awake.

That particular Sunday morning it was my mother-in-law hissing in my face and thrusting the phone receiver at me.

"It's your secretary and she's hysterical!"

I took the phone from her, still half-asleep. "What's up, Rita?"

Her voice was about two octaves higher than I'd ever heard it before. "It's Felton! We were watching USA Today on cable and they were doing this special on domestic vacation spots, you know, like places in the US you can go to kick back--"

I got impatient. "Cut to the chase, Rita."

"Well, they were talking about Coronado, and they showed this close-up of the bridge, and Felton was staring and staring, and all of the sudden he jumped up like a wild man and knocked me down and grabbed my keys and took off with my car!"

"Felton knocked you down?" The thought of tiny Felton flooring my Amazonian secretary struck me as funny.

"Rick, pull your head out! He was headed toward the *bridge!*"

"Oh. Oh, no." The light finally dawned. "Oh, *God*!"

* * *

We took Bree's new car, since it was blocking the driveway. I noticed with irritation that it ran much more smoothly than mine. Bree had been out in her garden working with Margaret, who, like her Grandma, rose at dawn, and she hadn't taken time to change—she looked like a GI ready for jungle combat. Her face was smudged and almost unrecognizable, and her hair stuck out in stiff punked-out wisps. It would have been funny if I hadn't been so scared.

When we pulled up onto the bridge I saw Rita's Cutlass. It was idling in the slow lane, not a great place for it to be, but at seven on a Sunday morning there wasn't a lot of traffic. Felton, wearing what looked like one of Rita's satin robes, was balanced on the railing of the bridge stock still, as if he were thinking about something very important. I pulled the Mustang over and sprang out toward him, shouting.

"Felton, for God's sake, get down from there!"

If he heard me he didn't give me any indication. I dashed toward him, arms outstretched to grab his ankles, but he took a measured step forward without looking around and disappeared off the side of the bridge.

I froze, in shock. Bree was immediately at my side, her eyes filled with disbelief. We stared at the space where Felton had been, neither of us able to fathom what had just happened. Guilt overwhelmed me. *If I hadn't just hired him, if I'd just taken him home with me instead of giving him to Rita, if I'd just had him committed last night!...*

"*Hot damn!*"

Bree and I looked at one another. The voice seemed to come from over the railing. We both rushed at once to the side of the bridge and peered over.

There was Felton, the old happy irrepressible Felton, squatting on the ledge, a grin splitting his face. He looked up in surprise.

"Rick! What in the world are you doing here?"

* * *

"Look at this thing. Is this *hot*, or what?" We were sitting down at the police station. Felton was eyeing with interest Rita's negligee, which he still had wrapped around him. Underneath it he seemed to be wearing nothing but boxer shorts and a dirty pair of argyle socks. The socks astonished me as much as the negligee. Felton never struck me as someone who would care much about the kind of socks he wore.

He held the silky material between his fingers and caressed it gingerly. "Hot," he said again. It was ruby red, like almost everything else Rita wore, and it hissed against his rough fingertips. He shook his head. "Do you think she really wears this to bed?"

"You should know, Felton," I said shortly. "You spent the weekend with her."

He looked confused. "Did I? I must have been drunk. Why would Rita want to take me home with her? She can't stand me."

Bree shook her head.

It hadn't taken the police long to show up; I guess the sight of a short man in a scarlet negligee balancing on the rail of the Coronado bridge is enough to startle anyone out of his complacency. Once Bree and I had pulled Felton back up on the bridge, the three of us had been promptly arrested for malicious mischief. Of course there'd been no one to call but Charlie, and Bree, still being angry with him, had refused. I'd had to call him myself, which was more than a little humiliating. Felton had voiced that it might be a good idea to call Rita, too, in case she was wondering where her nightgown was, but I'd been all out of calls by that time and Felton hadn't been able remember Rita's number anyway. Bree had phoned her folks to ask them to look out for the baby for a little while longer, so that was that. I would catch hell at the office tomorrow from an irate Rita, I knew, but there'd been nothing I could do about it.

Charlie had shown up eventually, looking more sheepish than usual. To his chagrin Bree wouldn't even look at him, and he'd made up for it by being unusually charming to Felton, whom only the night before he had called a moron for locking himself in our bathroom. The police were convinced that Felton and Bree and I were trying to play a belated Halloween joke, but Charlie had us released and he'd taken us to his office.

Now I was astounded to see change in Felton; all his former vigor and self-confidence seemed to be back in force. He was beaming from ear-to-ear, and I could swear he'd regained his old sexual energy and was even eyeing Bree lasciviously.

"I knew it! Something in my gut told me he wasn't dead! I knew it all along." Felton had gotten to his feet and was gesticulating wildly, and for a moment I wasn't sure he hadn't gone mad. Then I remembered that Bree had said almost exactly the same thing about the bridge just a few nights ago, and I wasn't so sure.

"I saw that picture on TV and it was like slow-motion, man, I mean, I saw the whole thing in my head! Perry runs to the railing, drops over, catches himself on the ledge! I follow him, but I did just what you did, Rick! I stood there staring at where he was, I didn't even run over to see if he'd hit the water! I just *assumed!* I made an ass of *you and me!*" he finished triumphantly.

Charlie smiled patiently. "You think Perry Sinker slid over the side and hid on the ledge?"

Felton nodded his head impatiently. "I just proved it, didn't I? If I could do it, then a great big athletic guy like Perry Sinker could!"

"But *why*?"

"Why?"

"The motive," Charlie said simply, "What was his motive?"

Felton thought for a moment. "Well, it's either sex or money. It's always one or the other."

Charlie raised his eyebrows skeptically. "How could pretending to be dead get you either one?"

Felton looked puzzled. "Maybe he was just trying to get away from Bakersfield."

"Then why would Bakersfield hire me to have him tailed?" I interjected.

Bree had been sitting over in the corner, perfectly silent. Now she stood up and walked over to us, nailing Charlie with her green eyes.

"Carl Bakersfield hired Richard because he wanted to make sure there was a witness to Perry's death. Since there wasn't going to be a body, didn't there have to be an eyewitness?" She turned around and went back to her chair to pick up her purse. What is it about women's purses? Women seem to be attached to them by some sort of radar. And they're always full of junk-- empty gum wrappers, tubes of lipstick, leftover movie tickets. Nothing the ordinary male of the species wouldn't find in his pocket and immediately throw into the trash.

Bree started for the door.

"Why would Carl want to do that?" Charlie asked cynically. Bree turned toward him coolly.

"If you were any kind of law enforcement officer," she said, "you would have asked him that at the time of the suicide.

119

Instead you endangered my husband's career and nearly drove Felton to the funny farm!"

Felton looked at Bree in alarm. "I don't think it was poor old Charlie's fault--"

She turned on him. "Poor old Charlie should keep his mind on business, if he has a mind left, instead of spending his middle age chasing skirts!"

Charlie winced. "Ouch!"

Bree looked at him as if he were beneath contempt, turned on her heel and left, slamming the door behind her. I gave Charlie an apologetic shrug.

Charlie looked sad. "Maybe she's right. Maybe I haven't been paying enough attention to my work."

Felton put his arm around Charlie's shoulders comfortingly. "Come on, Charlie, I'll buy ya a drink. I know this bar where the waitresses wear poodle skirts..."

CHAPTER SEVENTEEN

"What are you thinking about?" Rita asked.

I was staring out of the second-story window of my office, looking down at the dozens of tourists and business people who had moved into the Gas Lamp District since its renovation had begun ten years ago. Across the street was an expensive art gallery, positioned inexorably next door to a peep show. The mayor had been trying to intimidate the adult book and movie houses out of this area and draw in 'legitimate businesses', but there were a few stubborn holdouts from the old days. I knew the owner of that particular peep show, not because I frequented it on my lunch hour as did some of the legitimate businessmen in the building (even my father, on occasion), but because the firm had done a job for him last year. His name was Vern Sheffield, and he was known locally as a man with strong ties to the mob. He'd discovered at the age of sixty-two that he'd been adopted, and he'd been interested in finding his real mother. We'd tried to convince him to save his money, but he'd have none of it, and amazingly, we did track the old woman down, ensconced in a nursing home in Yuma. He'd immediately brought her to San Diego and set her up in a condo across the bay. His sentimentality astonished me. I knew for a fact he carried major artillery under that baggy trench coat he always wore, and I was glad to be on his good side.

I was thinking that there was no telling what sentiments a person carried in his heart, and that Bree's anger at Charlie had something to do with things I didn't understand and probably didn't want to understand, but I wasn't about to tell Rita that. Instead, I turned away from the window and stared at her hard. She had on a fuzzy knit dress, tight everywhere it was possible to be tight but expensive and well-tailored, in the usual blazing red. One black eyebrow was lifted as she looked at me. She still hadn't forgiven me for not calling her from the police station yesterday, but apparently Bree had told Helen to give her a ring, so she wasn't kept totally in the dark. Unfortunately, no one had seen Felton since he'd dropped Charlie off after an afternoon of carousing, and Rita wasn't convinced yet that he was back to his normal self. "Well?" she said, crossing her arms, her eyebrow climbing even higher.

"Did Delores Zapata ever mention Carl Bakersfield to you?"

"No. Why do you ask?"

"I think Felton may be onto something. I think Carl Bakersfield might have set me up. He needed a witness to Perry's suicide; he hired me and I hired Felton. I know Tracy didn't recommend me, and there are dozens of P.I.'s in the phone book. Why me?"

Rita smiled. "Because you're incompetent?"

I frowned. "Very funny." I wasn't sure she was trying to be funny. Perhaps Delores had told Carl that she'd hired me to find the twins, and that I hadn't had any luck. Of course, that didn't make me incompetent, but it might have looked that way to Carl.

But Delores didn't work for Carl anymore, hadn't for awhile. Instead maybe she'd mentioned me to Marilyn's mother, who'd told Marilyn. No, Marilyn had been in the South Pacific for several months.

Or had she?

Rita was still smiling at me. "Isn't it interesting," she said, reading my mind, "that Marilyn Cutter came back from an extended tour of the South Sea Islands just in time for her father's funeral?"

"Are she and Bakersfield still married officially?"

"As far as I know."

"Then any money she inherits will be his, too."

"Not necessarily. What about prenuptial agreements?"

I chewed on that a moment. "Of course, only his lawyer would know for sure," Rita said sweetly.

His lawyer.

Tracy.

"I'll get her on the phone," said Rita, starting back to her desk in the reception area.

I grabbed my coat off the coatrack. It was still freezing out. "Don't bother," I told her.

* * *

Tracy's office is only four blocks from mine, but the place is light years away stylistically. It's situated on the twenty-fifth floor of a brand new office building that houses some of the largest corporations in the country. Tracy had gone to work for Sullivan, Bradshaw and Bick right out of law school, and she'd been made a full partner three years ago. Her office alone was the size of mine, Dad's and Rita's combined. The carpet was immaculate, the view spectacular. Tracy, as usual, looked stunning, if you could ignore the smirk on her face.

"What the hell do you want? I'm busy."

She didn't look busy to me. Her desk was as clean as Charlie's, except instead of polished wood she had smoked glass, resting on two marble pedestals. Luckily I knew her secretary, Louise, fairly well; we'd grown up down the street from each other, and she, being a non-neurotic, mature adult, figured that my sister would naturally be happy to see me.

I casually positioned myself opposite Tracy in one of the four stuffed chairs facing her desk. I'll say this much for Tracy--her chairs are comfortable. I smiled at her winningly.

"I need some information."

"What makes you think I'm going to give you any information?"

"You could do it in the spirit of familial love."

"Ha!"

"All right. You could do it because if you don't do it I'll tell your husband and every voter in the city that I caught you with your pants dow--"

Her face caught fire. "That's over now! And you shouldn't have been there in the first place! I could probably have you arrested for--"

"Simmer down. Look." I tried to be reasonable, a good trick when I'm talking to Tracy. "You help me out, I'll help you out. That's what siblings are for, right?"

"I don't *know* what siblings are for! All I ever wanted in my life was to be an only child!"

"Well, you're not. So give."

She leaned back in her swivel chair, her face going slack. Even her swivel chair looked comfortable, I thought enviously. "What do you want to know?" she asked, her voice flat.

"Did Carl Bakersfield have a prenuptial agreement with Marilyn Cutter?"

Her color rose again. "That's not your goddamn case anymore--"

"Just shut up and tell me. I have my own reasons for asking, not the least of which is my liability in case Perry Sinker is *really* dead."

"What are you talking about? Of course Perry Sinker is really dead!"

"Felton gave the police a rather convincing argument to the contrary. Or doesn't your lover keep you informed of these developments?"

"Charlie is not my--"

"Did they or did they not have a prenuptial agreement?"

"No they didn't, not that it's any of your business!"

"No?" That answer took me by surprise. "Why not?"

Tracy sighed. "You always asked too many question. Even when you were little. You used to drive us all crazy..." She slumped forward, elbows on her desk, and rested her face on the heels of her hands. I couldn't imagine her doing this in front of a client, but then, I was just her idiot brother. I didn't count.

"I tried at the time of the marriage to convince Carl to draw up an agreement, but he said that Marilyn's family was just as well off as his and he didn't see the point of it. Even Perry--" She stopped suddenly, biting her tongue.

"You knew Perry Sinker?"

She hesitated. "Of course," she finally said, reluctantly. "Everyone who knew Carl knew Perry. Carl never went anyplace without him." She smiled slightly. "He was even best man at Carl's wedding."

"God! So what are you saying? Did Perry think Carl should have a prenuptial agreement?"

"Perry was against the marriage altogether, of course. He told Carl that it was just an infatuation, that it would pass, but Carl wanted to make Perry happy, and this seemed to be the only way."

I shook my head. "Wait a minute, what are you *talking* about? I'm totally confused now."

Tracy suddenly stood up firmly. "No. That's it. I'm not going to give you anything else. I've said too much already. There's such a thing as client confidentiality!" She set her jaw and I knew she'd made up her mind not to say anything else.

Her intercom buzzed abruptly. Tracy reached out a lacquered nail and pressed the button. "What is it, Louise?"

"Mr. Waxman is on the phone for you, Mrs. Lowe."

Tracy blushed, looking up at me guiltily. I grinned maliciously. "I thought that was all over with! Naughty, naughty!" I skinned one index finger over the other. Her eyes turned bright red and she picked up the nearest thing she could find, which was, unfortunately, a rather large pink quartz paperweight from the top of her desk.

"You--*brat*!" she screamed, hurling it viciously in my direction. Luckily she'd never been that athletic and the paperweight missed me by a good two feet, but it put a nice-sized dent in the wall just above her sofa.

I decided that discretion was the better part of valor and I ducked hurriedly out of Tracy's office. In the reception area, Louise looked up at me questioningly as I passed by, and I winked at her. As Bree said, some things never changed.

* * *

Marilyn Cutter was wearing a shiny, sky-blue leotard and beneath it her body was a supple as an eighteen-year-old's. I watched with envy as she bent her body backward and sent all six feet of herself soaring through the air in a flawless flip. Her trainer, a stocky gray-haired woman in her fifties, nodded approval. I stepped forward. Marilyn spotted me and jerked her head at the trainer, who eyed me suspiciously before she left. Marilyn threw a spotless white towel around her neck and brushed past me arrogantly, pushing her way through a swinging door. After a moment, realizing she wasn't going to come back, I followed.

The door led through a private dressing room with twenty or so tan-colored metal lockers. No one was there, but on the cement floor I found Marilyn's sky-blue leotard, dropped in a sweaty heap. I picked it up; a whiff of it reached me: a heady mix of perspiration and very expensive perfume, the kind that seems to emanate from the pores of rich girls. "Mrs. Bakersfield?" I called tentatively. "Marilyn?"

"*In here...*" I followed the voice through another door into a small sauna. It took a moment for me to spot her sitting on the single bench that snuggled against the far wall.

She was naked. Stark naked.

She smiled at me tauntingly. "What's the matter, Mr. Matthews? Afraid of a little skin?"

"No. Afraid of a *lot* of skin." Her golden tan seemed complete; as far as I could see she had no tan lines. Her ivory hair was soaked and plastered against her skull, and without make-up she looked even more formidable, a Nordic goddess in a vengeful mood.

"It's hot in here."

"Then take something off, Rick. Or don't you think your little wifey trusts you?" She closed her eyes and laid back on the bench, gracefully thrusting her long legs against the tile wall. It was an erotic pose and yet, at the same time, there was something so deliberate and cold about her that it made me remembered suddenly why I was there. I also knew that my little wifey wouldn't hesitate to take advantage in a similar situation.

"I need to ask you a few questions, Mrs. Bakersfield."

She frowned, her eyes still closed. "Don't call me that. Call me Mickey, if you want. I hate the name Marilyn. It reminds me of Marilyn Monroe, and she was such a weakling." She opened her eyes again, staring at me defiantly. "I'm anything but weak."

"I can see that."

"You can't yet, but you will. Now, what can I do for you? Not that it matters, of course. Carl intends to send you to the poor house, if he has his way. And he *always* has his way."

"Not always, apparently. *You* left him."

"Only temporarily. We both needed our space."

"But you're still living at your mother's house."

"Just until Daddy's will is read. Then Carl and I are planning to take a long cruise. Maybe you and your charming wife would like to come with us? She seems like *such* an interesting person. Minus the kid, of course."

"I doubt if Carl would like that."

She shrugged elegantly. "He's very tolerant of my--hobbies. He could be talked into it." The white towel was still hanging around her neck and she reached up with it and swabbed off her dripping forehead. "I like it *really hot* in here. I hope you're not too uncomfortable."

My suit had wilted but it didn't matter; it was due for a dry cleaning anyway.

"When did you first meet Perry Sinker?"

She thought about it for a moment. "Well, let's see. I believe I met Carl in Boston at the Cotillion. And of course Perry was there with him; Carl didn't go anywhere without Perry back then. I thought the two of them were quite an impressive pair."

"You have friends in Boston?"

"I have friends everywhere..." she smiled slightly.

"Was Perry from Boston too?"

"Perry was raised here, in San Diego, I think, though from what I was given to understand he'd traveled a great deal."

"You didn't get along with Perry."

Her eyes flashed suddenly. "Who told you that?"

"I have my sources."

"Well..." She seemed to collect herself. "Perry and I had our differences, it's true. It was a volatile situation, and of course, he was there first. But I wouldn't say we didn't get along. We had a lot in common."

"Carl, for instance?"

She smiled again, that feline smile, half-amusement, half-sneer. "You know, the whole world isn't middle-class, Mr. Matthews. Some people are more adventurous than others. And I can truthfully say I never let an opportunity pass me by..." She sat up languidly, leaned toward me, and pulled the towel from around her neck, tossing it casually to the floor. "Can you say the same thing?" She stood up slowly, fixing me hypnotically with her glacial eyes. I stepped back abruptly, hitting my head against the door. She pushed her golden skin against my soggy suit and pinned me to the wall. Her strength was amazing. "Come on, Rick..." she purred, claws clicking against the white tile, "...why not try a little something different?..."

She was squeezed up against me so hard that I had to gasp for breath. "I'm happy with what I've got, thank you."

She looked into my eyes critically for a moment, saw that she wasn't getting anywhere, and suddenly retreated. As she reached down to pick up her towel she mooned me; it was her parting shot. She wrapped the towel briskly around her middle.

"Men. You're a boring lot." She pushed me aside easily and stepped back into the dressing room. I followed her and a rush of cold air hit my hot, wet suit. I sneezed. Marilyn ignored me, pulling a plush white robe from one of the lockers and slinging it over her shoulders.

"Mrs. Bakersfield?"

She turned, eyes narrowing. "Are *you* still here?"

"Why did you marry Carl?"

She stared at me. "Persistent, aren't you? What's in it for you? Carl fired you, you won't get any money out of it."

"I'll learn the truth."

She scoffed. "There are as many versions of the truth as there are people to tell it. If you want to know why I married Carl Bakersfield, ask your wife." She started out the door.

I was perplexed. "What does *that* mean?" But when I stepped out into the gym again, she was already gone...

CHAPTER EIGHTEEN

My dad joined the Navy when he was eighteen. He'd been inspired, apparently, by a Gene Kelly musical, not to mention an overwhelming desire to get off the Nebraska farm where he'd been born and to see a little bit of the world. That was June of 1945, and by the time he'd been trained and shipped out, the war in the Pacific had ended. He had consequently been stationed at the Naval Base on Coronado Island, right across the bay from downtown San Diego. Twenty years later he'd retired from the Navy, but not from Coronado. He still owns the three-bedroom house he bought there in 1952 for $14,500, an exorbitant sum at the time. It is now worth well over $500,000, but he lives in it alone, with no intention of selling. He says that Tracy and I will inherit it when he dies, and he insists that it's a good investment, but I figure by that time Coronado, which sits at sea level, will be lost in the Great Quake, sunken off the continental shelf like so much sandpaper, for future generations to discover in their underwater explorations. I've often wondered what they'll make of Dad's collection of foreign beer cans lining the walls of the old family room. Or the piles of Golden Age comics he's saved from his boyhood and would never let me touch, even back when I was seven and fascinated by the vivid covers. "Those'll be worth something someday," he used to say, hiding them in the top of his closet where I couldn't reach them. He was right about *that*, and it was a good thing, too, because when it comes to money Dad has the instincts of a gopher. He's never been able to make ends meet and if it hadn't been for his navy pension, he would have spent his declining years begging for quarters in front of Horton Plaza. Consequently, when he has medical problems, he always finds himself on the seventh floor of the Veteran's Administration Hospital.

I have nothing against the Veteran's Administration. I find that it is not less competently run than, say, the Post Office, or any other government funded facility. But that isn't saying much.

Dad was presently ensconced on a ward with fifteen other sickly veterans, a kind of barracks set-up with gauze curtains to pull around the beds for privacy. Nobody ever pulled the curtains, of course, and when you visited you were likely to see things you would just as soon have not seen. Dad was sitting up in bed with a thermometer in his mouth when I arrived; Mom was seated on a stuffed chair beside his bed, occupying herself with some elaborate needlework. Dad had a peptic frown on his face, as if he'd swallowed something bitter, but Mom was all smiles when she saw me, showing that dimple I had loved so much as a child. She looked terrific; she is just this side of sixty but can pass for fifty easily; she's tanned and tall and slim and her blue eyes shine merrily. When I was a kid she'd been a knockout, and I'd never been able to figure out why Dad had felt compelled to roam. He didn't know a good thing when he had it.

I filled him in now on the latest developments with Bakersfield. When he heard that I was wasting my time on a case we weren't being paid for, his frown deepened and his face turned slightly greener, but he didn't say anything. Mom offered to walk me to the elevator.

"He's got a perforated ulcer," she murmured. "Dr. Clayton is trying to make up his mind whether to operate or just to change his diet and try to let him heal on his own."

"It's nice of you to look after him like this, Mom."

"I thought so," she answered.

"So what's Jason think of his wife running off to the hospital with her ex?"

"Jason is in South Hampton at the moment," she said primly, "and not likely to be back soon. But since you asked: your father called me in agony. He said he needed me. How could I refuse?"

"Just say no?"

She smiled indulgently and pinched my cheek. "I'm quite old enough to take care of myself, thank you. Tell Bree I said hello, and give the baby a kiss for me!"

She breezed down the hallway back toward my father's room, her bobbed silver hair swaying. I made a mental note to invite her for dinner while Bree's folks were here. I got into the elevator and started down. The only other occupant was a wheezing relic in a wheelchair. I looked at him. He winked at me, grinning a toothless grin. "Vietnam?" he said politely.

"I'm just visiting."

"World War I, m'self. Took some flak in the groin. Ain't been the same since. Pee m' bed every night." He grinned again. "Got rid of three wives that way. Faithless bitches, one and all."

The elevator door opened. I said a silent prayer of thanks and stepped out into the lobby, just in time to spot Charlie coming out of the administration office, his arms filled with files. He looked up and saw me and as he caught up to me he smiled timidly, no doubt remembering our last encounter.

"Bree still mad at me?" he asked sheepishly.

"I wouldn't know. What do you have there?"

He showed me the file on top. "Well, Felton got me thinking that maybe Perry Sinker really *didn't* go off the bridge. In that case he might be a candidate for the skeleton in the wall." I frowned at him, not following. "Dental records. Also medical--I did a little research. Perry served in Iraq before his slight brushes with the law. Wanna have a look?"

* * *

We drove over to Charlie's apartment in Point Loma. It's positioned at the top of the hill overlooking the ocean, and Charlie takes full advantage of the view. The apartment is in a brand new building, but the landlady, like every other woman in the city, adores Charlie and lets him have the place for half what its other occupants had paid before him. Charlie had moved there about six months ago, and I'd never seen the apartment, but since we were only a few minutes away, it seemed like a smart idea to look over the files there. Besides, we were both hungry by this time and Charlie, I knew, could grill a steak just short of perfection, so I decided to let him. I phoned Bree from his place to let her know I was going to be late, but the machine was on. Naturally we'd both forgotten our cell phones: she hated hers and I was just sloppy. Bree had talked about taking her parents to Old Town today--maybe they just weren't back. I wanted to check the answering machine to see if Felton had called, but I could never remember the code. Numbers always elude me. I have a hard enough time remembering my home phone number.

Charlie was in the kitchen, singing the second verse of "Oklahoma" at the top of his lungs as he fried up our steaks, relentlessly cheery, as usual. I sat on his sofa, a white Danish modern piece that would have lasted exactly two minutes around my house, and thumbed through the files on the glass coffee table before me, noting how similar Charlie's tastes were to Tracy's. How he ended up with Bree originally, I'll ever know. Bree's idea of decorating was a trip to Tijuana to see if she could find a ceramic Popeye figure to match the one of Wimpy she already had.

Perry's VA records indicated that he had spent almost seven months of a two-year hitch in the Army ensconced in the VA Hospital in San Diego with a virulent case of tuberculosis, which he'd apparently contracted during basic training. Also, he was thirty-six now, not twenty-seven, as Carl had indicated to me. But, of course, Perry had probably lied to Carl about his age.

"Soup's on," Charlie called from the kitchen, which was immaculate, as was the rest of the place, even though Charlie had just spent half an hour in there whipping up dinner, which included sautéed onions and a micro-waved baked potato. He'd set the small kitchen table with red-checked cloth napkins and a couple of teak salad bowls, and he was scooping some sort of spinach salad into mine as I seated myself. I noticed a copy of Bree's latest book, *Mood Over Miami*, lying on his counter.

"Did Bree give that to you?"

"No," Charlie admitted ruefully as he sat down. "I went out and bought it, full price. She's really outdone herself with this one; have you read it?"

I shook my head with irritation. Charlie laughed, stuffing salad in his face. "That's right, you never read *any* of them."

"She's never even *been* to Miami."

"Miami's the name of the villain, not the town. Maybe you should give it a try. It's dedicated to you, you know."

"No thanks," I answered sullenly. "What I don't know can't hurt me."

Charlie stared at me, frowning. "You amaze me, Rick. I can't figure out why you became a private detective! You're the least curious person I've ever known."

"I'm curious about other people's lives. But I'm not particularly interested in a deep psychological analysis of my own, so let's drop this, huh?"

Charlie sensed my annoyance and lifted his hands. "Okay, okay! I didn't mean to touch a nerve!" I reddened guiltily. "So what did you find in the folders?"

"Not much," I admitted. "Perry had TB ten years ago. He got a medical discharge from the Army."

Charlie nodded. "I'll take the file in to the coroner. Maybe he can match the dental records." We looked at each other, sensing somehow that this wasn't going to happen.

* * *

I got home around seven pm. The door was locked, and it took me a good five minutes to persuade the key to turn. I could hear Lester in the backyard howling furiously at what he took for an intruder, but I had completely forgotten about Waffles, who sunk his teeth into my ankle the minute I stepped over the threshold. I kicked him away, but one thing you learn about dachshunds is that they're as tenacious as bulldogs, and he came charging back despite the tiny cast on his leg, skittering across the hardwood floor, his long nails making little grooves in the finish. Luckily there is a coat closet right next to the front door and I was able to open it and, using my leg like a hockey stick, shove Waffles into the closet and slam the door shut before he injured me further. For a moment I guess he was too surprised to even whimper; then he started to bark, loudly and furiously. I walked back into the kitchen, shutting the doors between us as I went. One thing I like about old houses: every room has a door. I could hardly hear him back there. After ten minutes he left off barking abruptly, as if he'd run out of gas. I was pretty sure he hadn't asphyxiated, since it was a big closet, but just to make sure I went and stood by the door, my ear pressed against it. I heard canine snoring. I went back to the kitchen and got myself a glass of iced tea.

Bree pulled up in her new Mustang about fifteen minutes later, disgorging Helen and Hugo and, amazingly, Felton. Bree took Margaret out of the car seat, waving gaily at me through the kitchen window. Helen seemed to have bought every serape she could find, and she was carrying a pair of red-and-orange leather cowboy boots. Hugo was wearing a genuine Mexican sombrero, black velvet with silver trim. On a lesser man it might have looked ridiculous, but somehow it fit his personality, which was oversized anyway. Felton spotted me peering out of the window and grinned wildly, bursting with good will. He helped Helen carry her stash into the house, almost hidden behind an enormous mountain of souvenirs; then he headed straight back to the kitchen.

"Where have you been?" I asked him sourly.

"Old Town, with Bree's folks. Nice people. And you wouldn't believe the babe that sold us those boots!" Felton whistled low and long, leaving little doubt as to the salesgirl's attributes. "Made a date for eight, so I can't stick around!" He turned, heading through the swinging door toward the living room.

"Hold it, Felton! You were scheduled to see the court psychiatrist today, remember?

Felton patted my shoulder solicitously. "I saw him this morning, Rick. Don't worry! He gave me a clean bill of health, said I was as sane as he was."

I looked at him doubtfully. He glanced at his watch. "Listen, buddy, I'm going to be late. I'll see you in court tomorrow afternoon, okay? Bye, Helen, bye, Hugo!" he said as he danced out the front door. They waved to him cheerily. Bree came out of the baby's room, looking wiped out. "The baby's down. I'm going to try to get a little work done."

"Whatever you want, dear," Helen answered patiently. "Now don't worry about us. We can entertain ourselves, can't we, Daddy?" Hugo put a big paw around my shoulder. "Ever try Mexican beer, son?" he asked me, pulling a six-pack out of a woven bag and shoving a warm bottle into my hand.

Helen looked around curiously. "I wonder where Waffles has gotten off to?"

* * *

Bree came to bed around two a.m. She had moved her computer into our dining room during her parents' visit and I could hear her *tap tap tapping* at the keys, but the day had worn me out and I was sound asleep already when she got under the covers, dressed in my pajamas. Her feet were ice cold and when they touched my wounded ankle I shot up, bumping my head against the end table.

"Sorry..." she whispered. "...I didn't mean to wake you."

"That's okay," I answered sleepily. "What were you working on?"

"Just some notes...for my article..."

She started to fade away but I wasn't quite ready to let that one go.

"You mean the article for *The Reader*?"

"*Mmm-hmmm...*"

"Bree, wake up! I want to talk to you about this!"

"*Shhhh*! Richard, for heaven's sake, it's two in the morning. Can't it wait?"

"I don't like the idea of you doing that article!"

"You've made that perfectly clear."

Silence.

"Well?" I said finally.

"Well what?"

"Don't you care what I think?"

She leaned up on her elbow then. The light from the still-full moon was coming in through the wooden shutters on the bay windows, giving her skin a pale, ethereal glow.

"I care what you think, of course. I just don't let your opinion rule my life. I have to care what *I* think more. That's reasonable, isn't it?"

"I don't want you to be reasonable! I want you to be my *wife*!"

She frowned slightly. "I *am* your wife. I'm willing to discuss this logically with you. But ultimately it's my decision. Right?"

I squirmed uncomfortably, a spring piercing my spine. She had me, really; there was no way I could object to her article without looking like a jerk. I turned away from her, trying in vain to get comfortable. Apparently she thought the question was settled and she snuggled up spoon-like against my back, her knees nesting behind mine. Her breathing began to slow almost immediately.

"Bree?"

"*Hmmm*?

"Why did Marilyn Cutter marry Carl Bakersfield?"

A deep sigh. "She married him for money."

"What? How can *that* be? The Cutter family is loaded!"

"Not Carl's money. *Hers*. Her father disapproved of her-- extracurricular activities. His will specified that unless she married with his consent, she wouldn't inherit a dime."

"But why Carl?"

"His pedigree checked out and Mr. Cutter was convinced that Carl wasn't a fortune hunter. It worked out for them both." Bree yawned widely.

"For Marilyn, anyway. But I don't see what Carl got out of it. He couldn't have been in love with her, and he already had money... Bree, are you still awake?"

Her voice was muffled and irritated. "No thanks to *you*..."

"I don't get it. What did Carl get out of it?"

"Who filed the missing person's report on Marilyn? Think about it."

I thought about it for a minute. "Perry Sinker. Perry? Are you trying to tell me you think Carl married Marilyn because *Perry wanted her*? Oh my God!" The room seemed suddenly to light up. *Perry*! Tracy had said that Carl would have done anything for Perry, and Marilyn's father would never have approved of her marriage to a bisexual jailbird! That *had* to be it! This was getting more and more interesting. Perry Sinker in love with Marilyn Cutter, their constant fights, Carl's solicitude, her desertion! Motive enough for suicide, perhaps. Or better yet, *murder.*

Suddenly I could hardly wait to get to the office tomorrow and have a look at the Bakersfield file...

LIE LIKE A WOMAN

CHAPTER NINETEEN

I was limping a little as I walked up the wide wooden staircase to my office the next morning. My bitten ankle had swollen during the night and it was puffy and red, and I thought seriously about stopping in at the doctor's office for a tetanus shot on my way into work, but something in the back of my mind propelled me directly to the Gas Lamp. Maybe it was a premonition, I don't know.

Rita was lying on the floor of the waiting room when I got there, her glossy black hair resting in a puddle of blood. There was so much blood that at first I thought she must be dead, but after a moment she opened her eyes and looked up at me and smiled wryly. "That's what I get for coming to work early," she said weakly as I helped her to her feet. The gash on her forehead wasn't even deep; whatever she'd been hit with had glanced off her temple, knocking her out without causing any permanent damage. The office had, however, sustained serious injury. There was not a piece of furniture left unturned. The file cabinets had been emptied out and the papers scattered from one end of the room to the other. Both my office and Dad's had been similarly abused, and I noted with satisfaction that someone had managed to break my desk chair, so at least I had an excuse to find myself something more comfortable.

"Whoever it was must have been waiting behind the door when I opened it," Rita muttered. "Look at this mess!"

"I'd better call Charlie. Somebody was looking for something." I started picking up files, sorting through them to see if I could find Perry Sinker's photograph, I but gave up after a few minutes. It was hopeless in this disaster. Rita had a lot of work ahead of her.

We washed the blood from Rita's cut and I borrowed a band aid from the superintendent, who refused to lend me one until I assured him that we weren't going to sue the owners of the building for faulty security. I put in a call to Charlie and he came right over, bringing with him a couple of youngsters in uniform that reminded me of myself ten years ago.

The only thing I had ever really liked about Rita was that she was totally apathetic to Charlie's charm, and today, as always, she treated him with rude indifference, answering his questions in a monotone and rushing through their interview. Charlie could never understand her dislike of him, and today he went out of his way to be ingratiating, but it was useless. The two rookies dusted the place for fingerprints and ogled Rita, who, even with a band aid on her forehead and blood drying dark brown on her crimson dress, was an undeniable eyeful.

I gave her the day off, even offering to drop her at her apartment, but she waved me away and said she'd be back in an hour, after she changed her clothes. Charlie shook his head as he watched her sashay down the stairs. "I don't know what she's got against me..." he mourned. He turned back to me. "Have you noticed whether anything is missing, anything valuable?"

I shrugged. "Who can tell in this mess? Besides, we don't keep anything valuable at the office."

"No firearms?"

"Are you kidding? I don't even carry a gun, and the only one registered to the firm is in the safe at Dad's house."

Charlie considered for a moment. "Maybe you should think about getting it. Whoever broke in here didn't think twice about bashing Rita--he might have a grudge against you."

"I doubt it," I said shortly. "I'm too innocuous for anyone to form a grudge. We do divorces, not felonies."

"So far..." Charlie dismissed his rookies and together we headed out the door, not bothering to lock it, since the lock had been broken with a crowbar anyway.

Charlie strung a short piece of yellow police tape across the entrance. "Do you think that will keep them out?" he asked me, laughing.

* * *

As Felton's court-appointed guardian, I was required to make an appearance at the inquest. Charlie said he'd like to come along, even though I'd warned him that Tracy would be there. He was uncharacteristically mum on the subject as we walked up the sidewalk to the courthouse. Maybe it really *was* over between them, but it was much more likely that Tracy intimidated Charlie as much as she did me.

Felton was standing with Mel Farley, the bailiff, as we walked into the courthouse; they were both bent over double, guffawing over one of Mel's raunchier jokes, no doubt. Felton looked terrific. He was freshly shaven and he looked like he had actually put on a few pounds in the last couple of days. His suit, for once, was spotless and unrumpled; Rita had sent it off to the dry cleaners while he was her houseguest, which explained why he had been wearing her negligee. His eyes sparkled with the old enthusiasm, and he slapped my arm when he saw me. "Well, Rick, old buddy, ready to face the Philistines?"

The Philistines were waiting inside the courtroom in the form of my sister Tracy and Carl Bakersfield, who were sitting together at a small oak table in front of the courtroom, implacably huddled together. Tracy's eyes widened when she saw Charlie, but I couldn't tell whether she was pleased or displeased. Her reaction to Felton was not so equivocal. She wrinkled her nose in disgust at the sight of him and turned back to Carl, whispering in his ear as he nodded. Charlie and I sat down on the opposite side of the courtroom, and Charlie stared longingly at the back of Tracy's head all the way through the inquest.

Judge Ratchett entered the courtroom unceremoniously. Simon Wischerath, poised uncertainly at his table, jumped up immediately when he saw the judge, and hastily called Felton to the stand. Felton trotted jauntily through the gate, actually flashing Tracy a smile and a wave as he took his seat. Judge Ratchett looked at him. Felton grinned.

"Has this man been examined by the court psychiatrist?" the judge asked Simon sternly.

"Yes, your honor. I have the report right here." Simon stepped up and nervously handed a folder to Judge Ratchett, who looked at it for a moment, then handed it back. The judge leaned backward in his chair, folded his hands across his formidable stomach, and shut his eyes wearily. "You may proceed..."

These were the words Simon lived for. He pushed his glasses up onto the bridge of his nose and leaned over the stand toward Felton, locking eyes with him. In his best Perry Mason voice he asked: "Where were you on the morning of October 27th of this year?"

"Tailing Perry Sinker."

"'Tailing him'? Please explain that term to the court."

Judge Ratchett leaned back even further. His chair made a loud creak of protest. "Mr. Wischerath," he said, without opening his eyes, "we all know what that means."

Simon colored slightly. "Yes, your honor." He turned back to Felton. "Is it true that you followed Perry Sinker onto the Coronado Bridge, where he parked his car?"

"Yes it is."

"And is it true that you watched as he got out of the car and ran to the rail?"

"Yes it is."

"And is it true that you saw Perry Sinker throw himself into the San Diego Bay?"

Felton grinned even wider. "Nope!"

Judge Ratchett opened his eyes. "Nope?"

"Nope! I saw him go over the rail. But I never saw him hit the water."

Judge Ratchett looked puzzled. "You mean you were too late to see him actually drown?"

Felton leaned toward the judge confidentially. "Naw! He never drowned! There's this ledge under the bridge, see, and he just hid under there till we all left!"

Tracy was on her feet instantly. "I object, your Honor! Conclusion on the part of the witness! Did he see Perry Sinker hiding under the bridge?"

"Sit down, Mrs. Lowe! This isn't a trial." Ratchett turned back to Felton. "Did you?"

"Nope. But I didn't see him hit the water, either. And if he drowned, where's the body?"

The judge raised an eyebrow. He looked over at Tracy skeptically. "Just how do you go about selecting your witnesses, Mrs. Lowe? I'm interested."

"Judge, this man is obviously deranged! Last week he was blaming himself for Mr. Sinker's death, and now he claims he didn't *witness* it!"

Without a word Judge Ratchett gathered his voluminous robes about him and stepped down from the bench. He turned as he started back toward his chambers, fixing Tracy with his fierce brown eyes. "Don't waste my time!" he snarled. Tracy turned pale. Ratchett pushed through the door, slamming it angrily behind him.

We all stared after him for a moment, flabbergasted; then the court began to buzz. Carl Bakersfield was stunned. He began to whisper in Tracy's ear, gesticulating furiously.

Felton looked sweetly at Simon Wischerath. "Am I done now?"

Simon nodded, blowing out a breath and shaking his head. Carl and Tracy stood up simultaneously, and they both rushed toward the exit. Charlie called after Tracy as she was leaving, but she didn't turn around.

* * *

"This isn't Perry Sinker," said Granger Spoon flatly as he leaned over the table, upon which the recovered skeleton laid, yellowing and silent. Granger held a lower mandible in his hands as he spoke, and he pointed to the back teeth. "See this? The wisdom teeth never erupted. According to this chart, Perry Sinker had all his wisdom teeth extracted when he was nineteen."

Granger put the mandible down and started stripping off his gloves. His iron-gray hair hung in a greasy lank down his back, caught up in a red rubber band. He was an old hippie who had somehow managed to earn a Ph.D. in forensics. He worked for the police department mostly, but he also managed to teach an occasional class at the University in La Jolla, which was where Bree had met him years ago. Bree was a great favorite of his; as a student she used to haunt his lab. I don't think has ever forgiven either Charlie or me for marrying her, but he was doing his best to be civil to us as we watched him work.

"You're sure about that fact?" Charlie asked him sternly, attempting to light his pipe for the hundredth time that afternoon. Granger blew out Charlie's lighter, frowning with disgust.

"Don't smoke in here! You know better than that!"

Charlie pocketed the pipe. "Sorry..." he said sheepishly.

Granger pulled off his latex gloves and tossed them unceremoniously into a tin trash can, then he moved over to his metal desk. On the wall behind it were pinned charts illustrating various workings of the human body: labeled skeletons, circulatory systems, bones of the hands and feet. Granger didn't offer us a chair, but I sat down anyway on a footstool beside the examining table. The unidentified skull sat at the end of the table, staring at me with its deep eye sockets. I stared back. Granger noticed and smiled.

"They have a character all their own, don't they? Looks like he could almost talk to you."

"What else indicates that this isn't Perry's skeleton?" I asked, trying not to stare into those empty sockets.

Granger thought about it for a moment. "Well, Perry Sinker had TB. That causes bone damage. This skeleton shows no indication of that. And Perry Sinker's records indicate that he'd sustained a broken nose during his basic training."

"No broken nose?"

"No broken *anything*. Of course, I don't have the whole skeleton," he said sarcastically. "Someone misplaced the little finger bones..."

Charlie cleared his throat. "We'd better go, Rick."

Granger didn't bother to see us out. We were already out the door and in the hall when I heard him yell, "Hey, Rick! Tell Bree her new book's terrific! She learned something from me after all!"

More than we did, apparently.

* * *

Judge Ratchett had leaked to the press that the case of Perry Sinker's disappearance was not closed after all, due to the inefficiency of certain lawyers, and by the time I returned to the office that evening, Tracy had already called six times in a state of high dungeon. That was pretty much Tracy's natural state when it came to me anyway, so I ignored the messages. With her usual skill Rita had hired a temporary secretary to help her, and already the office floor had been cleaned of both loose papers and blood spills. The little secretary, a Mexican girl named Wanda, sat at Rita's desk, sorting through unorganized material. When I came through the door she looked up and smiled brilliantly, then spoke to Rita in Spanish. Rita answered her, chuckling.

I followed Rita into my office, shutting the door behind me. Rita smirked.

"She thinks you're cute."

"Doesn't she know any English?"

Rita shook her head. "She's just over the border. Only been here a week."

"She's an *illegal*?" I said, a little panicked. All I needed was an arrest for employing illegal aliens.

Rita nodded. "Don't worry, you're not taking advantage of her. I'm giving her a good salary."

"I'm not worried about *her*!" I growled, noticing with irritation that Rita had also had my old chair fixed while I was gone. I sat down uncomfortably. "Did you find Perry Sinker's glossy?"

"No. It's missing. In fact, the whole file is missing."

"Anything else gone?"

"Not that I could say, but it's hard to tell." She moved over to the window, pressing her eyes shut with her long tapering fingertips.

"How's your head?" I asked her. "Want me to take you to the doctor?" She did look a little paler than usual.

"Just a little headache. I'm fine. Delores Zapata is coming by first thing tomorrow morning with her husband. If it's okay with you, I think I'll take off now. I want to go visit your Dad in the hospital." She looked at me, a slight frown between her eyes, and I noticed for the first time that she was wearing a black sheath; skintight, true, but black nonetheless.

"Did somebody die?" I said curiously, indicating the dress.

"Not yet," she said ominously, "although that guy who bopped me had better watch out!" She left without further ado. I realized that it was almost eight p.m. and, shepherding Wanda out the door, I locked up. Rita had gotten the door fixed and had outfitted it with a new lock; Wanda produced the key with a little grin. She was at most eighteen, and by the way her black eyes flashed when she looked at me, I knew I was in for some trouble. My Spanish is terrible, but there are some things you don't need words for. I dropped her off at her bus stop and headed home to Bree.

CHAPTER TWENTY

I was dreaming that Bree and I had been stranded together on a tropical island. The palms swayed above us and the warm waves rushed in just inches from where we lay, supine, on the burning sand. Bree lounged beneath me, a silken sarong draped over her soft curves. She looked up at me languidly and began to emerge from the silk like a butterfly from a cocoon. I held my breath. Above us in the trees the tropical birds sang sweetly, except for one annoying magpie that emitted a trill like the sound of a *ringing phone--*

Bree jabbed me in the ribs with her elbow. "Richard! Answer it before the baby wakes up!"

I came to with a start. It was still dark, and the phone was shrilling next to my ear. I grabbed the receiver as Bree sat up on the mattress beside me, her expression a mixture of irritation and curiosity.

"Hello?"

"Is this Rick Matthews?" A prepubescent voice.

"Yes? Who is this?"

"You're such a dumb ass! I tole you Perry Sinker didn't drown himself!"

I covered the receiver and turned to Bree. "It's that kid again!" I said in a frantic whisper. She stared at me for a moment, then leaned over and started fooling with the answering machine. In another second I heard a click as the tape started rolling. I uncovered the receiver.

"It's four a.m. If you want me to keep talking to you, you'd better tell me who you are." There was a faint echo as I heard my own voice being recorded. I held my breath, hoping the kid wouldn't hang up.

"You know who I am, moron!" the kid hissed, guffawing. *"Some private eye!"* At this point the kid whispered an aside, and I heard a giggle. *"You'd better get us out of this, dumbshit, or you'll be sorry! We don't trust them anymore. I overheard them talking about getting rid of us!"*

"Who?"

"You know!"

I sighed. "This is getting monotonous. If you can't be more specific I'm hanging up."

Another aside from the kid; I could barely hear him saying to someone on the other end, *"He wants us to do all the work!"* Then there was silence. For a second I thought he'd hung up; then he said, *"We're at the big house."* There was a rustling, like he'd dropped the phone, and an angry, deep voice. I couldn't make out words, but then there was a crash, and the dial tone buzzed in my ear.

I hung up, turning to Bree. "Did you catch any of that?"

She nodded. "Barely. I didn't want to turn up the volume. Do you think it's a hoax?"

"Do *you*?"

She considered. "Maybe you should run the tape by Charlie, see what he thinks. I don't like the way things are going, with your office being broke into and Rita hurt that way. You might be next."

I smiled. "Are you worried about me?" She nodded sweetly and I pushed her gently down onto the mattress and kissed her, snuggling as close as I could. Her skin was hot and melting, and, although her pajamas were not exactly a silk sarong, she still emerged from them with the grace of a butterfly...

* * *

Everyone was in the kitchen when I got up the next morning, even though it was still fairly early. Helen had virtually taken over the cooking, and I was beginning to miss Bree's excursions into the exotic. Bacon and eggs were the limit of Helen's breakfast attempts, but Waffles didn't seem to mind. He .was greedily gulping down the remains of Bree's meal as Bree sat at the kitchen table, staring out the window listlessly as her mother talked.

"--and Audrey's boys just *love* them! There's nothing wrong with a little Coca-Cola now and then--"

"It's full of caffeine--" Bree muttered under her breath.

"--and Audrey *always* put it in their bottles when the boys had stomach aches--"

I saw Bree wince. Margaret was sitting in her high chair, hanging onto her grandma's every word. I took a piece of bacon off Margaret's plate, kissed her tangled cloud of hair, and headed out the backdoor. Bree handed me Margaret's yellow plastic tape deck, the one with the painted ladybugs.

"You'll need this. Did you remember the cassette?"

"Right here." I patted my coat pocket, then winked at her and blew her a kiss. She blushed slightly, knowing I had taken advantage of her last night, but unable to scold me in front of her mother, who, still quite oblivious, was launching onto another topic.

"Now your brother, Scott--"

* * *

Wanda was sitting at Rita's desk when I came in, polishing her fingernails with a repellent-smelling violet lacquer. She glanced up at me when I opened the door, then she hastily stored the polish in the top drawer and shot me a seductive smile. Suddenly she noticed Margaret's tape recorder in my hand, and she started to giggle with embarrassment. I stuck the tape deck behind my back, frowning at her.

"Ah--" I had taken three years of Spanish in high school, but I'd spent most of my classes daydreaming about Lila, a girl I'd had a crush on, although, in four years, I'd never got up the nerve to ask out. "*Donde esta* Rita?" I asked Wanda slowly, my accent exceedingly lame. Wanda took my broken Spanish as a sign of encouragement and flashed her brilliant white teeth. "*Esta aqui*," she said, pointing to the door of my office. I nodded my thanks to her and went into my office, where Rita was already sitting with Delores Zapata and her husband Fred. I guess Rita figured they deserved *something* for their money, even if it was only the pleasure of her company.

Fred stood up and shook my hand, his expression chagrined. He was sporting a black eye, and I got the impression that it wasn't the result of a bar fight.

"Sorry I rammed yer car like that!" he said solemnly. "I was outta my mind with jealousy. Couldn't help m'self." He seemed extremely humble. I slapped him on the shoulder.

"It's understandable, Mr. Zapata. These things happen." Delores sat primly at her husband's side, her face unreadable. He watched her uncomfortably, clearing his throat. "Ya see, Mr. Matthews, we done run outta money and we can't afford to pay you no more...I got laid off m'job, and, well, that's that." Fred sat down, letting out his breath in relief. His accent, which was deep Texas, like Delores', threw me, but I remembered that Rita had told me long ago that Delores and her husband were second-generation Mexican-American who'd migrated recently from San Antonio. I was alarmed to see tears welling up in Delores' dark eyes.

"I don't want you to worry about a thing. I'll keep working on the case *por gratis*."

Fred looked at me suspiciously. "For *what*?"

"That means for free."

"We don't take no charity," mumbled Delores, "even if we *are* poor!"

"It's not charity, Mrs. Zapata. You've overpaid me as it is. Don't worry about a thing." I sat down on my chair gingerly, not certain it wouldn't splinter into pieces, and I looked over to Rita. She was staring at Margaret's plastic tape recorder with fascination. "Rita, did you find the Zapata file?"

"Right in front of you," Rita answered, still staring at the tape deck. She reached down and pressed the PLAY button. A tinny rendition of "*The Eensy Weensy Spider*" came on. Rita grinned at me. "Expanding our musical vocabulary, are we?"

"Turn that off!"

She pressed the STOP button.

I opened the file and started looking through it. "Let's just go over a couple of things, Mrs. Zapata, now that we know this isn't a case of spousal kidnapping."

Delores looked at me blankly.

"We know Fred didn't take the twins."

Delores nodded.

"And you're sure they didn't run away?"

"They was *good boys*!" Delores said fiercely. "They *loved* their mother!"

"I'm sure they did, Mrs. Zapata, but apparently they have a bit of a juvenile record. From what I can tell, they've spent more time in juvenile hall than they have at home. Breaking-and-entering, malicious mischief…" Apparently last summer the Zapata twins had made a stink bomb that ended up emptying out Balboa Theatre on the fourth of July.

"They never *runned* away! They was *taken*!"

"Okay, okay, I believe you. When was the last time you saw them?"

"I told you already!"

"Refresh my memory, please."

Delores was clearly disgusted with me, but she sighed and gave in. "I *told* you. I was cleaning houses that day. It was a Thursday, my busiest day. Them boys was with me, foolin' around with their chemistry set. I told them they couldn't take it with them but they never listened. Anyway, after I cleaned the big house I took 'em to wait for the bus, and when I got on I realized they was missing--"

I was suddenly struck. "What did you say?"

"They was *missing*," Delores shouted impatiently. "Ain't I made that clear?"

Fred piped up wearily. "We gotta keep goin' over this? I got a bowling league tournament in half an hour!"

"Delores, did you say the *big house*?"

"That's jest what we call it. You know. Miz Bakersfield's son's house."

I was dumbstruck. I reached into my pocket for the phone message tape and tossed it to Rita. "Play this."

Fred groaned. "I'm gonna be *late--*"

Rita took off "*The Eensy Weensy Spider*" and stuck on the tape we'd recorded in the answering machine the night before: "*I'm sorry, we're not able to answer the phone right now--*"

"Forward it!"

Rita pressed the button. My voice came on mid-sentence. "*--you want me to keep talking to you, you'd better tell me who you are...*"

"Is this a joke?" Delores asked, not amused.

Then the reedy, childish alto: "*You know who I am, moron!*" Delores stood up suddenly, her face dead white, and then she fell operatically to the floor in a faint. Rita jabbed the STOP button and rushed to the outer office for a glass of water. Fred cried out as if he'd been shot.

"You done *kilt* her!" I knelt beside Delores and managed to raise her head, no easy task considering her bulk. She opened her eyes and looked at me.

"It was Lonnie!" she cried. She jumped up from the floor with amazing agility and rushed to Margaret's tape player, nearly knocking down Rita, who had entered with a paper cup full of water. Lonnie's voice came on again. "*--You'd better get us out of this, dumbshit, or you'll be sorry! We don't trust them anymore. I overheard them talking about getting rid of us!*"

Delores gasped angrily. "Somebody wants to get rid of my boys?"

Fred nudged her. "Hush up, Delores, I can't hear what they're saying!" They both hushed.

"*--can't be more specific I'm hanging up.*" My voice. Delores and Fred shot dagger eyes at me for daring to threaten to hang up on poor little Lonnie.

The whispered aside. "*He wants us to do all the work!*" The giggle. Then: "*We're at the big house--*" Now we all listened, wide-eyed, at the crash, then the loud angry voice. It sounded much more ominous knowing what I now knew. I thought Delores would faint again, but she didn't. She leaned against old

Fred's shoulder and shut her eyes. "*He's* got them," she whispered in horror.

"Who?"

Delores opened her eyes wide and stared sightlessly at me. "*Carl Bakersfield.*"

CHAPTER TWENTY-ONE

Charlie looked at me from across his shiny, clutter-free oak desk.

"You want me to arrest Carl Bakersfield for kidnapping?"

"You heard the tape! Delores swears that's her son Lonnie's voice! What more do you need?"

"Evidence of a crime, for starters." Charlie leaned back in his swivel chair and tapped tobacco into the cup of his briarwood pipe. He applied his lighter and sucked, but the tobacco was not the least bit interested in burning. Apparently this didn't bother Charlie. He put the lighter back into his vest pocket and continued to puff periodically on the pipe, even though no smoke appeared.

"Rick, I'm sure you believe what you're saying, but the truth is that Lonnie and Donnie Zapata each have juvenile records as long as your arm. I question the wisdom of arresting a prominent socialite for the kidnapping of two young hoodlums who could probably eat him for breakfast without swallowing."

"But the tape--"

"No one said a *word* on that tape about Carl Bakersfield. It sounded to me like a not-very-funny prank played by a couple of prepubescent delinquents."

"They said they were at the Big House!"

Charlie smiled patiently. "Maybe they meant Sing-Sing." He could see I was not amused. "Listen, Rick, no offense, but you're taking this case awfully seriously considering that you got thrown off of it weeks ago. Those two Zapata brats will turn up, like bad pennies; if they were five years older they'd be in federal prison for some of their escapades! Their parents should be thankful they're gone."

"That's very humane of you, Charlie."

"I tell the truth, that's all."

"Are you sure?"

He blinked. "What do you mean?"

I stood up, glaring at him. "How long have we known each other, Charlie? Six years, seven?"

"Something like that."

"Do I strike you as being a frivolous person?"

"Not at all." Charlie puffed, watching me.

"Then do it as a favor to me. Make up some excuse. All I want to do is search Carl's house!"

He shook his head. "Sorry. I can't."

"You mean you *won't*! Maybe you're afraid of offending a certain lady lawyer we both know..."

Charlie stared at me. "You don't believe that."

"Don't I?"

He leaned forward, folding his hands on his desk, surveying me with kind gray eyes. "I would never, *never* let my personal feelings for anyone interfere with my duty as a police officer." He reached a beefy hand out and patted my shoulder fraternally. "You've been under a strain, Rick. Things haven't been going your way lately. Do yourself a favor. Go home, see the wife and kid, spend some time with the folks. Things will look brighter in a bit."

"Quit bugging you, you mean."

He laughed. "Hey, you couldn't bug me even if you tried, Rick. What are friends for?"

* * *

That was the question on my mind when I got home at lunchtime, but I soon forgot it. Helen greeted me at the door, apron in place, Margaret wrapped protectively in her arms. Margaret was obviously ready for a nap; her face was smeared with grime and she kept rubbing her sleepy blue eyes. Helen was perturbed about something; a mixture of anger and frustration stamped her features and she flung open the front door before I could even get my key in the lock.

"I want you to know--" she hissed, "--that I don't approve of these kinds of goings on, not in the least, especially with a *child* in the house!"

Before I could ask her what she was talking about, she'd hustled the baby into her nursery and slammed the door. I could hear the rocking chair squeaking in rhythm to Helen's slightly off-key rendition of "Rudolph, the Red Nose Reindeer".

In the dining room, Hugo was sitting silently at Bree's computer keyboard, staring balefully at a nonsensical configuration on the screen. Bree's computer manual was lying open beside him, exactly where he'd had it since breakfast. He didn't smile when he saw me.

"I hate this machine..." he muttered.

"Where's Bree?" I asked politely.

He pointed toward the back at the house and started fooling with the keyboard again. "Damn!" he growled. I walked through the kitchen toward the French doors in the back.

Waffles, who was resting as close to the refrigerator as canine-ly possible, growled when he saw me, but he didn't move. His belly was enormously distended and he probably found it impossible to move, even for the pleasure of inflicting pain upon me.

I slipped out discretely into the backyard. Lester seemed to be sulking in his doghouse, which was almost as large as a seaside cottage. He ignored me, as usual.

"Bree?" I called.

"In here..." came a muffled reply from the garage.

Our garage is the detached kind, virtually useless for storing a car, but rather handy if you need a shed. Today Bree was using it as a shed. She had propped a large flat piece of plywood up between two sawhorses, and she was perched on a high rickety stool next to it. Piled on this makeshift table were sculpting tools of various sorts, a large mound of pinkish clay, about three dozen pencil erasers, three or four variously shaded wigs, several calipers, four pairs of glass eyes: blue, green, brown and hazel, and one of her old college forensics textbooks.

And a human skull.

Bree turned and flashed me a brilliant smile. "How's my hunk?" she purred, her mood generous.

"Deflated," I said flatly. It was dark in the garage except for a single bare bulb that hung down a cord directly above the table. I went over and picked up the skull, staring into those familiar soulful sockets.

"Does Granger know you've got this thing?"

"Granger gave it to me. It's not the original anyway, it's just a plaster cast. Granger called to see if I wanted a crack at reconstructing the face, and I said yes, if I can do it by hand. I hate the computer program the department uses—lacks soul...." She plucked the skull from my hand gently and set it down beside her sculpting tools.

"Have you done this before?"

"Twice. Had pretty good luck with it both times; the department made positive identifications from my work. Of course that doesn't count college--we had to do one for our final in forensic anthropology." She picked up a caliper and made a delicate measurement, jotting it down on a lined pad at her side. "I don't think Mother approves of me fooling around with bones. She never did like my interest in crime."

"That didn't seem to deter you."

She shrugged. "She had Audrey and Scott to intimidate. Every family needs at least one black sheep."

"Yeah. I should know."

Bree looked up at me and grinned affectionately. "You're hardly a black sheep, Richard. Maybe a little gray around the edges." She looked at me more closely now and frowned. "What's the matter, honey?" she said softly.

"Remember that tape? The one we made last night of that prank phone call?"

She nodded.

"Well, Delores Zapata swears that that's Lonnie's voice on the tape, and that the Big House refers to Carl Bakersfield's place."

Bree's eyes lit. "Bakersfield has the boys! My God!"

"That's what *I* think. But Charlie says there's no real evidence to support that theory and he refuses to give me a search warrant. He thinks I need a vacation."

At the mention of Charlie's name, Bree's face clouded. "Charlie's working off his own agenda on this one..." she said with irritation. She turned back to the skull, taking another measurement. Then she picked up one of the erasers, cut it in half, and carefully cemented it to the bottom mandible.

I hadn't the faintest idea what she was doing.

"Bree?"

She looked up.

"What do you think I should do about this?"

She smiled slightly. "Well, Richard, you know me. I never let legalities stand in the way of my pursuit of justice. If you want a job done, sometimes you have to do it yourself..." She turned back to the skull. I pondered this remark for a bit.

"How long is it going to take you to finish that thing?"

"Three or four days. If I'm not interrupted too often." She grinned. "Don't you have work to do?"

I grinned back, leaning down and kissing the top of her auburn head. Then I headed for the door.

"Richard?"

I turned back to her.

"Don't get caught," she said without looking up.

* * *

There comes a time in every case when a detective, if he's any kind of detective at all, has to make a leap of faith, even though others stand mired in the sludge of evidence. That time for me was *now*. If I were a female I'd chalk it up to women's intuition; when Bree does it, she calls it a hunch, and she does it *regularly,* with much less evidence than I had now. I knew Carl Bakersfield was holding the Zapata twins; if I could get into his house, I could find out *why*.

I needed someone to go with me, someone who wouldn't ask too many questions, someone with skills I didn't have, someone possessing unquestioning loyalty. But who?

* * *

For as long as I can remember, Felton has lived in a transient hotel downtown on Sixth Street and Dover. He refuses to find a real apartment, even though he can afford it now, because he says he wants to stay footloose and fancy-free, whatever the hell *that* means. I hadn't been down to his place in over a year, and I was startled to find as I drove down Sixth that *The Swans*, Felton's hotel, had been renovated in keeping with the renaissance of downtown San Diego. Where once there were exposed bricks and stains of indeterminate origin, now there was a salmon-and-turquoise plaster facade with a sign announcing the name of his hotel in shocking pink neon letters. The lobby, formerly littered with winos clutching brown paper bags, now boasted peacock-patterned theater carpeting and green velvet turn-of-the-century furniture. The winos had apparently been ordered to their rooms or back onto the streets; the smell of urine was barely detectable. It wouldn't be long before the post-yuppies took over this building and raised the rents. Soon all the indigents who had lived here for decades would be crowding the park at Horton Plaza. Already it was crammed with humanity and the homeless were becoming aggressive, some even, in their desperation, attacking tourists, who are the lifeblood of this city. There had to be a solution. I'm all for urban renewal, but things have to be renewed for *everybody,* not just for the privileged few who can afford it. How rich to you have to be? How much is enough? I'm one of those people who can't be happy with what I've got unless everyone's got as much as I have. It just doesn't seem fair otherwise; no one works that much harder than anyone else. And putting in more hours is not working harder, contrary to popular belief. Even Felton would be out on his francis before long. True, Felton could afford something better. It was doubtful the rest of them could...

Felton was still in bed when I knocked on his door; he wasn't sleeping, just engaged in watching "The Young and the Restless" on his tiny color set with an intensity I've rarely seen in him. I was relieved to find that his studio apartment was just as disgusting as it had been the last time I'd been here. The walls were still the same scabrous yellow and the decaying carpet showed a scarred hardwood floor that pre-dated World War II. Felton's laundry, if you could call it that, was piled behind the only chair in the place, an overstuffed relic that was useless anyway, since it was virtually hidden beneath Felton's famous collection of overdue parking tickets. Since the hotel had no parking lot, Felton usually simply parked The Bobsled from Hell any old place he could find. There must have been at least a thousand dollars in Felton's overdue fines heaped on that chair. It was a small miracle that he wasn't in jail.

The soap opera ended and Felton hopped nimbly out of bed. Apparently he slept in his jockey shorts and those amazing argyle socks he'd been wearing on the bridge. He yanked on a pair of stiff blue jeans, then reached behind the chair, picking up a single shirt at a time and sniffing each one. None of them seemed to please him. He opened his tiny closet door. Wedged inside the closet was a bird's eye maple bureau, the only decent piece of furniture in the room. Felton stuck his hand into the top drawer and took out a striped cotton dress shirt, still in its original wrapper. As he pulled the cellophane off of it and extracted the pins, his attention turned to me.

"Rick," he began, his look beatific, "I'm in love at last!"

"The salesgirl from Old Town?"

He nodded his head enthusiastically. "I know it's hard to believe, but she's everything I ever wanted in a woman!" He pulled on the shirt, wincing when a missed pin pierced his neck. He reached up gingerly and worked the offending pin loose. "Only one trouble, though..."

"She's a transvestite?" I guessed cynically. I'd seen Felton in love before, and in my experience it was a temporary state of affairs at best.

"She's under-aged."

"How under-aged?"

He shrugged. "Oh...fourteen?"

"*What!*"

"I swear to you, Rick, she looks twenty if she looks a day! I had no idea she was such a kid when I asked her out!"

"Well, you can forget it if you think I'm going to visit you in the penitentiary! Between this and Perry's jump off the bridge and that mountain of traffic tickets--"

His face dropped. "I know, I know...Tracy's out to get me as it is..."

I clapped him on the back. "Better find yourself a nice divorcee, Felton. With two children, preferably."

Felton slumped on the bed again. "You're right, you're right...I gotta keep my nose clean..." He looked up at me expectantly. "What is it you wanted, Rick?"

* * *

The Big House was located on the edge of an embankment overlooking the ocean in Sunset Cliffs, a rich man's area that can't make up its mind whether it is part of La Jolla or part of Pacific Beach. The property surrounding it occupied about five acres of prime Southern California real estate, and the house itself was enormous, twice the size of the Cutter place, although not a fiftieth its age; Carl Bakersfield had had this house custom-built a mere two years earlier. It took me and Felton half an hour to figure out that there was no way to traverse the eight-foot-high stone wall that surrounded the entire property in front, and that the only way for us to reach the house was from the beach, up the cliff on steep steps that had been carved there decades before. Public access to this particular beach was four miles away in La Jolla Village, so I drove my car to the main drag and parked it in the post office parking lot: then Felton and I carefully climbed down an incredibly steep embankment to the tidal pools, and we started walking south along the coast.

I hadn't counted on having an afternoon in the sand, and my shoes, Espirit loafers, just weren't cut out for this kind of activity. Felton was wearing the same pair of running shoes he'd been wearing when I met him, and he didn't seem to be having any trouble, but the sides of my loafers were too low, and every half mile or so I'd have to stop and shake the grit out. Not to mention that I seldom wore these shoes and the soles were stiff. They hurt my arch, which was too high, anyway.

"What if Carl's at home?" Felton wanted to know.

"He's not. His butler told me that Carl and Marilyn have gone sailing on her yacht for the next couple of days. They won't be back till the weekend."

"How'd you find that out?" asked Felton admiringly.

"I pretended I was calling from Tracy's office, told the butler she had some papers for Carl to sign."

Felton chuckled. "Tracy will be so *pissed* at you when she finds out!"

I snorted. "Tracy has a list of things she's pissed at me about that dates back twenty-five years! This little indiscretion will hardly make a dent."

I took in a deep breath. It was a gorgeous day, for a change, although it was still quite chilly, and I was tempted to do what Charlie suggested and just relax and watch the sea gulls circle overhead. Then one of the unsanitary little buggers let loose and soiled the shoulder of my sport jacket. Felton thought this was pretty funny, but to me it was a sign to keep my mind on business. I was trying to wipe the residue off my suit with a discarded ice cream wrapper when Felton looked up and pointed.

"Hey, isn't that Carl's place?"

Sure enough, we had walked all four miles without realizing it. We started up the steps toward his house, which loomed like a brilliant white temple above us. The steps were well-worn; although probably not by Carl himself, whose sandy hair and freckles seemed primed for sunburn. More likely it was Marilyn who had used them, I thought, remembering her golden skin. For a moment I considered telling Felton about my steam room encounter with Marilyn, but I vetoed the idea. The last time I told Felton anything intimate, a story that involved an embarrassing incident in a drug store when I was fifteen, he'd spread it to everyone we knew, including Bree. Felton loves to gossip.

I wondered why Carl would leave the back part of his property unfenced when he took such pains to protect the front part. Then halfway up the cliff, I knew. No burglar in his right mind would attempt to climb these steps--you could have a coronary just trying to get to your objective. Every four or five steps I had to stop to catch my breath.

"What you need is a Stairmaster, Rick!" Felton volunteered. "Build up the lungs! Too much sitting behind the desk is bad for the old ticker!" I noticed with exasperation that Felton, who was older than me and half my size, was barely breathing hard. I resolved to join the gym down the street--if I ever got paid again.

We started back up the steps.

"How do we know the butler's not here?"

I sighed, not wanting to use up my precious oxygen supply. "It's his afternoon off." When we reached the top, we stepped over a small ledge onto the greenest, lushest lawn I've ever seen. Felton, awed, leaned over and plucked a sliver of grass. "Is this stuff real?"

I nodded. "Chem-Lawn." The backyard was as impressive as most municipal parks I've seen. In the center of it all was an enormous swimming pool, but it didn't look like a regular pool. Instead, the builder had used stones and plants to make it look exactly like a hidden lagoon. The water was a soft, seductive blue-green, like the Mediterranean. A waterfall tinkled at one end, completing the effect. Felton's eyes were big as saucers. I was afraid he would rip off his clothes and plunge in at any moment, so I steered him toward the row of French doors that lined the patio. On one of them was a decal that said:

THIS PROPERTY IS PROTECTED BY
ANDERSON SECURITY SYSTEMS

I looked at Felton. "What do you think?"

He smirked. "Piece of cake." After his stint as a security guard at the college, Felton had worked for a few months in electronic home security systems. He told me once he'd taken the job just in case he ever decided to commit himself to a life of crime, but I suspect the real reason had something to do with his inability to qualify for the police force. No one cared how tall he was in security systems, and Felton had a knack with electronics. He'd fixed my stereo more than once.

"Want to give it a whirl?"

Felton winked at me, then he disappeared around the corner of the house. When he came back ten minutes later, he produced a shoe horn from his pocket and, slipping it past the lock, he opened up the French doors.

Together we stepped through the doors into the sun porch. I say 'sun porch' because there's no other way to describe it. A riot of plants filled every corner; a hammock hung suspended between two trees planted securely in enormous marble pots. In the center of the room was an elevated koi pond, filled with dozens of multicolored exotic fish so huge and tame that they swam to the edge of the water to be petted like so many scaly cats. I had to drag Felton away; he was fascinated with them.

"Do you think they could survive in a bathtub?" he wondered.

"Not *your* bathtub," I remarked shortly, anxious to find what we were looking for and get the hell out of there. The sun porch opened up into an enormous living room. The decor was sparse and Japanese, with white Berber carpeting that actually crawled up onto the seating platforms. Very minimalist. I tried to imagine Perry Sinker's fifties furniture fitting in here. No wonder Carl had stored it in his warehouse.

Then it suddenly occurred to me as we walked from room to gargantuan room that there was not a single book to be seen anywhere. Our home in Kensington has more books than furniture in it. Most houses have at least Reader's Digest condensations. Perry's books, stored in the warehouse, must have numbered in the thousands. I mentioned this to Felton, who shrugged.

"I'm a big reader but I don't own any books."

"How do you read, then?"

"The library. It's free."

I frowned. "I doubt if money is an object with the Bakersfields..."

Felton looked at me as if I were crazy. "They're rich, aren't they? Money's *always* an object to the rich! If they cared about anything else, they wouldn't be *rich*, would they?"

It made a certain kind of sense. Felton turned a corner and broke into a happy grin. "Look! A kitchen!"

Through the swinging steel doors before us loomed the largest kitchen I'd ever seen, a stainless wonder that smelled as if it had never been used.

"You could roller skate in here!" Felton marveled. Every surface was spotless; there wasn't a crumb in there big enough for an ant. Felton ambled across the smooth tile floor to a huge, restaurant-style refrigerator and pulled open the door. The interior was completely empty. He looked over to me, raised an eyebrow. I shrugged.

"Maybe Marilyn doesn't cook," I said.

"Oh, she *cooks*," Felton answered knowingly. "Just not *food*!"

We found a door that led into what looked like a study, with a beautifully-carved pink-and-black Italian marble fireplace, and placed in front of it, an ebony desk with a matching marble tabletop. I rifled through the desk drawers but they were bare. I was beginning to wonder if anyone really *lived* here. There was no evidence of any personal belongings that I could find, and certainly nothing to indicate that there had ever been children here, much less children as destructive as Carmen Zapata's little cherubs.

"Let's look upstairs," Felton suggested. "Maybe he's got the twins tied up."

It took us twenty minutes to find the spiral staircase that rose out of one of the back rooms up into the west wing of the second story. The second story itself had four wings made up entirely of bedrooms and adjoining bathrooms. The bedrooms were all exactly alike: king-sized beds on black lacquer platforms with minimal black lacquer furnishings and displays of quality artwork. Whoever had decorated may not have liked books, but he *loved* paintings. The closets were as large as my living room, and vacant. Each adjoining bathroom was the size of a spa, and contained not only a working hot tub, but a glass-enclosed combination shower-and-steam room. The porcelain was a glossy black and the fixtures were painted with red enamel.

We had searched three wings and were just about to go down the hall of the fourth when I was suddenly struck with the certainty that the Zapata twins were gone.

"They're not here, Felton. Let's go."

166

He looked at me in disbelief. "What are you talking about? You risked my reputation on a break-and-enter and you're telling me now that they're not here? Are you *crazy*?"

"I just have a feeling that they're already gone. Maybe Carl and Marilyn took them on the boat--"

"--and dropped them in the bay."

We looked at each other.

A sudden moan came from down the hall. We both jumped. "My God!" Felton whispered. "That's *them*!"

Another moan, more like a whimper this time. "They may be hurt!" he cried. "Carl probably *tortured* them!"

"Don't get melodramatic, Felton," I said testily, but he was already creeping stealthily down the hallway toward pitiful sound. I followed him reluctantly. There was something eerily familiar about that whimpering, but I couldn't put my finger on what it was.

As we approached a closed door at the end of the hallway, the whimpering grew into a blatant whine. Felton, seized with an attack of heroism, pressed onward.

"It's all right!" he shouted through the door, "We're here! We'll save you!"

He put his shoulder to the door and shoved. It opened inward easily. We stood there in the hallway a moment, wide-eyed, staring into the dark room beyond the door jam, but we couldn't make out anything but blank space. The whimper came again from below. Felton and I glanced down at our feet simultaneously. On the floor in front of the door stood a brandy-colored miniature dachshund, staring angrily up at us, its fangs bared. Its whimper turned suddenly into a low, insidious growl.

"Oh, *look*," said Felton, relieved, "It's just a little *doggie*! *Good doggie*!" Before I could warn him, Felton had reached down to pet it, and the good doggie sunk its sharp little teeth into Felton's right palm until they met. Felton shrieked and started shaking his hand, but the beast locked its jaw on his bleeding flesh and wouldn't let go. I tried to pry its mouth open, but Felton was screaming and hopping up and down so fast that I couldn't get a firm enough grip. I finally got hold of its tail and twisted. It let go of Felton and fixed its beady little black eyes on

167

me. I held it up by its tail and Felton, clutching his mangled hand, shot out of range and found the nearest closet, where he ensconced himself. A snarl started in the back of the little monster's throat, and I dropped it hastily and backed away. It launched itself at my trouser leg, tearing away fabric and a portion of flesh. I ran into the doorway. It leapt at me in a frenzy. I slammed the door between us and heard a thud as its brainpan hit the wood. For a moment I didn't hear anything; I prayed silently that the little fiend had knocked itself out when it hit the door.

Then the howling started, like something from a bad horror movie. No doubt the little beast was infuriated that it hadn't been able to obtain its human meal; not *yet*, anyway.

Felton was still in the closet, probably bleeding to death. I had to do *something*. I ran across the hallway to one of the other identically-decorated bedrooms and ripped the scarlet comforter from its bed. Then I dragged it back across the hall and, holding it in front of me like a net, steeled myself and opened the door.

The little brandy-colored dachshund leapt into the air, making a lunge for my throat, and I threw the comforter over it, gathering the cloth together at the bottom. The comforter was probably too thick for the little beast to bite through, but I wasn't taking any chances; as far as I was concerned, this dog was as dangerous as a rattlesnake, and less amiable. I tossed the makeshift sack over my shoulder, Santa-style, and trudged back to the other bedroom. The little creature, inexorably trapped now, snarled and snapped to no avail. I tossed the bag, dachshund and all, into the other bedroom's closet and slammed the door hastily. Almost as soon as the bundle hit the floor the little dog managed to escape, and I heard its minuscule skull crunch viciously against the wood. Its yapping was beginning to annoy me. As far as I was concerned, dachshunds were deadlier than pit bulls, and I began to compose a letter in my head to the American Kennel Association reprimanding them for allowing such a vicious breed to exist. The little beast escalated its vocalizations. "*Shut up!*" I shouted. It stopped for a moment, probably dumbfounded by my audacity; then it started yelping again, its voice hoarse.

I found my way back across the hallway into the room where we'd been attacked. The dog had distracted me so much that I hadn't realized that this room was different from the rest of the house. Amazingly, this room looked *lived it*. The bed was king-sized and black-lacquered, like the others, but it had been slept in, and there were items of feminine clothing draped over the chairs, and perfume bottles littering the dresser top. I went through the drawers and found pantyhose and some sheer and lacy underwear, not all of which was meant to cover. I could feel my cheeks burning. That perfume. *The kind that emanates from rich girls' pores...*

Marilyn's room.

I opened a large black wardrobe beside the bed and felt faint suddenly. It was filled with wigs of every shape and color, all sitting on wig stands, but not ordinary Styrofoam wig stands like the kind you see at your local beauty supply store. These particular wig stands were each and every one exact replicas of Marilyn Cutter's head.

It was startling, to say the least.

Suddenly I remembered Felton. I hadn't heard a sound from him and I was a little afraid that he might have bled to death by now. I ran over to the closet and threw open the door, expecting to find him unconscious on the floor. Instead, he was standing there staring straight at me, his hands behind his back, with a big shit-eating grin on his face. I pulled him out of the closet, which was filled to bursting with Marilyn's clothing. An entire wall rack held nothing but bright shoes and accessories.

"Felton, are you all right?"

He just stared at me, grinning.

"Felton, you're in shock! We've got to get you to the hospital!"

He refused to move; he just stood there, grinning like an idiot. I grabbed his right hand, which was dripping blood on the carpet. It wasn't as badly wounded as I thought it had been, but it definitely needed stitches.

"Come on! Let's go!"

I tried to pull him, but he wouldn't budge. He just continued to grin. "Guess what I've got in my other hand, Rick."

I stared at him blankly.

"It's a *key*! Get it? A key to our *case*!" He giggled.

"Felton, *please*!" I was beginning to get seriously worried.

"You don't wanna guess? Okay, I'll *show* you!" He happily stuck out his left hand. It was holding an expensive Italian men's loafer, the kind I couldn't afford in a million years.

"So?"

He shoved it at me like some demented shoe salesman. "Go on! *Take* it!"

"It's not my size."

He gave me a look that questioned my intelligence. Then, very patiently, he turned the loafer over and showed me its rubber sole.

Stuck to the sole was a big wad of green chewing gum. Which someone had tried, not very successfully, to scrape it off...

In the distance, the brandy-colored dachshund barked again.

It took me a minute to figure it out. When I finally did, I wanted to kiss Felton.

"Perry...the bridge...he was wearing it on the *bridge*!"

Felton nodded cheerfully. "You *got* it, chum!" Only Felton would notice a man in a loafer stepping on a wad of green gum. Thank God for Felton.

"Is the other one in there?" Felton reached back into the closet and pulled out the mate. I looked at him. "You know, of course, that no one else will think this proves anything, don't you?"

"Yeah, but *we* know, don't we? If Perry's shoes didn't go into the drink, then neither did Perry." He winked at me. I had to laugh. He was covered with blood and he looked as if he had been fighting dragons all day, but he was the old Felton.

We gathered up the loafers and started out the door. The dachshund, hearing us go down the hallway, erupted in a renewed frenzy.

Felton looked at me and smiled. "I love this work, don't you?"

CHAPTER TWENTY-TWO

Rita and Wanda were just closing up the office when Felton and I arrived. Felton's injuries were graver than I'd first suspected--not only did he require a tetanus shot and twenty-two stitches, but the dachshund had also broken seven bones in his left hand, and Felton ended up wearing a splint that splayed his fingers out like a paralyzed starfish. I wound up having to have a tetanus shot, too, which was just as well considering that I'd been attacked by Waffles earlier in the week, and who knew where *he'd* been? Rita inspected Felton's damaged hand gravely, but Wanda was concerned only with me. I'd done absolutely nothing to encourage her interest, but she persisted in fixing me with her black eyes, flashing periodic seductive smiles. She was not at all shy about it, either. Rita thought it was a tremendous hoot. Even Felton noticed.

"That kid's got the hots for you, Rick," he whispered enviously. "You better make sure Bree doesn't find out!"

"Bree wouldn't care if she did find out. Besides, Wanda's just a child and she doesn't speak English and I'm perfectly happy at home, thank you!"

Rita laughed. "The only living specimen of monogamous male in the Western hemisphere!"

Wanda, not understanding a word, laughed too. Soon everyone but me was laughing uproariously.

"I don't suppose you did any work here today?" I asked Rita sarcastically.

"As a matter of fact, I did." She airily handed me a piece of paper. It looked like an invoice to me, from Frutti Construction, Inc.

"What's this?"

"It's a copy of the work order for the construction, or should I say *deconstruction*, of Perry Sinker's house on Adams Avenue. Notice anything?"

I looked at it carefully. On it was some sort of blueprint of the house, along with a lot of indecipherable scribbling. I couldn't make heads or tails of it.

"I give up."

Rita smiled smugly. "Well, for one thing, the wall with the skeleton in it was never supposed to be touched."

That hit me. "The contractor made a mistake?"

"And he's paying through the nose for it. Carl threatened to take over his company and fire him if he told the truth about their contract."

I looked at her suspiciously. "Then why did he tell *you?*"

"What makes you think *he* told me?"

"Who did, then?"

"His wife. At the Laundromat. One thing you should have learned a long time ago is that wives are a much more reliable source of information than their husbands." Rita put on her jacket, a gorgeous scarlet silk trench coat that must have set her back four or five hundred dollars. "For instance," she continued, "I know from your wife that her ex-husband and your sister Tracy are planning to get a restraining order to keep you away from Carl Bakersfield and his lovely spouse if you come within a mile of either them or their property again."

"Great! That's great!"

Rita turned and gave Wanda an order in Spanish. Wanda immediately put on her own worn, ill-fitting cloth coat. They started out the door. Rita turned back to me, her expression softening somewhat.

"And something else...I figured this out by myself. Within a week this company is going to be in the hole if we don't get some clients in here. Maybe it's time to throw in the proverbial towel on this case."

I looked at her angrily. That wasn't what I wanted to hear. "What's the matter, Rita? Afraid you won't be able to find another job?"

She smiled slightly. "No, Rick. I'm afraid *you* won't..."

* * *

I decided to take Felton home with me, since it was my fault that he was injured. Helen had fixed a good old-fashioned brisket-and-mashed-potatoes dinner, and since Felton is left-handed, she spoon-fed him the entire meal. Margaret, who was used to getting most of Grandma's attention, did not take kindly to the situation, but Felton was in hog heaven. After dinner Hugo broke out the Mexican beer and a couple of cigars, and he and Felton retired to the back patio to smoke, despite the cold.

Bree was still in the garage working on the missing link when Helen handed me a plate of food to take out to her.

"I don't understand what she's doing out there with that--*thing*!" Helen fumed.

"Solving a crime," I ventured.

"Not very feminine work, if you ask me! And not a very good example to set for her poor little daughter!"

Bree's poor little daughter was, at the moment, sitting in front of our television set, gleefully watching Arnold Schwarzenegger annihilate a squadron of alien soldiers.

"She doesn't seem to be suffering," I observed.

"It's only a matter of time," Helen exclaimed, setting a platter of sliced meat on the floor in front of Waffles, who wolfed it down with savage enthusiasm.

Bree was not nearly as enthusiastic about *her* meal. She ate the mashed potatoes but refused the meat.

"What's the matter?" I asked.

"I don't know...I'm feeling a little green..."

"Maybe you should abandon the skull for now." The object in question was sitting in front of her on the crowded makeshift table. Bree had started applying the clay to it in pink strips that resembled muscles, according to some formula regarding the density of bone in the skull. The results were not exactly appetizing. It looked as if some poor soul had been beheaded and then flayed, which was enough to make *anyone* consider vegetarianism.

Bree looked as if she might faint at any moment. She'd never been squeamish and I was worried about her.

"Why don't you go lie down for a bit, sweetie?"

She ignored this advice and continued attaching strips of clay to the plaster casting. "I guess Rita told you about the injunction."

"Yeah. Good old Tracy. I'd like to know what I did to get on her shit list."

Bree smiled weakly. "You're male. She wanted a sister."

"She wanted a *father*. Is it *my* fault Dad abandoned her?"

"He abandoned you, too, but you don't hate the world for it," she said reasonably.

"Yeah, but I'm awfully suspicious of it." The garage was stuffy and the smell of the clay was beginning to overwhelm me.

"Bree?"

"*Hmmm?*"

"Do you think I should give up on this case?"

"What do *you* think?"

I rubbed my chin. I needed a shave; it had been a long day. "I think that Delores Zapata has the right to know where her boys are, and I think Carl Bakersfield has that information."

"But you can't get near Carl or Marilyn, can you?"

She looked up at me, her clear green eyes calm, expectant. She saw an answer, but she would wait until I saw it too; that was the way Bree was. It was one of the things I loved about her; she respected me enough to not talk down to me.

I looked down at the skull, then up at her, grinning.

"Maybe not Carl or Marilyn, but nobody ever said I couldn't get near Perry Sinker!"

Bree smiled at me, pleased. She took an old striped dishcloth from the table, moistened it, and covered the skull. Then she stood up, stretched, and kissed me, a long, hard, wet one. It wasn't often these days I got a kiss like that and I kissed her back, hoping that no one with a cigar would pop through the door. Outside on the patio I could hear Felton and Hugo debating the merits of the Padres vs. the Royals.

I looked down into Bree's sleepy eyes. "How are you feeling?"

"Better...I'm going to bed now. Want to come?"

How could I refuse an offer like that?

LIE LIKE A WOMAN

CHAPTER TWENTY-THREE

"He *lied* to us."

I was sitting on a chair at the VA hospital beside Dad's bed, waiting, while Mom dealt with the bureaucracy. It turned out that Dr. Clayton, the generic wonder, had decided not to operate after all. Dad was being discharged with a load of Pepto-Bismol and orders to stay away from the office until his symptoms cleared up. The way things were going, I figured that might be quite a while.

"He lied to us right from the *beginning!*" Dad shouted, banging his fist against his palm theatrically. A withered old veteran in the next bed turned and stared at us. I tried to calm Dad down, knowing that his ulcer wasn't benefiting from this display.

"It doesn't matter, Dad. I'm just going to assume from now on that anything Carl Bakersfield told us was a lie. You just go on home and relax, I'll take care of the whole thing."

Dad looked at me doubtfully.

"Really, it's all under control." Mom showed up with a wheelchair and a smile.

"Ready, Richie?"

At the sound of her voice, his whole demeanor changed. His eyes got soft and misty and the lines in his face disappeared.

"I'm ready, Dorothy..."

Mom helped him into the wheelchair and tucked an afghan around his skinny legs.

"Please come by to visit him, Rick. He's always happy to see you!" She started pushing him down the hall, just as if they hadn't been divorced for the last twenty-five years.

* * *

It was easy to assume that what Carl told us was a lie; the difficult part was remembering exactly what he *had* told us. The file on him had disappeared in the robbery at the office, and the only thing I knew for sure, thanks to Charlie, was the information we had gleaned from the VA hospital file on Perry Sinker. I also knew that Rita had dug up Perry's arrest record, with his single conviction. I had asked her to bring up the file again on the computer; the first copy she'd made for me had been stored in the Bakersfield file when it was stolen.

"Look at *this*. Funny we didn't notice it before," Rita said as she handed me the print-out. She pointed. I looked.

Perry's single conviction had been on an arson charge.

Rita frowned. "No other arrests for arson. Usually that's a repeat crime."

"How do you know so much about it?"

She smirked at me. "I read. You should try it sometime."

"All right. So he served seven months for arson. What'd he burn down?"

"Good question. Don't you have a friend on the police force?" Rita murmured sarcastically. "Maybe you could call in a favor."

* * *

Charlie wasn't in his office when I dropped by that afternoon. Since it was neither lunchtime nor quitting time, I asked around, and I found out that he'd left early without telling anyone where he was going. I had my suspicions, so I took the trolley back to the Gas Lamp and walked the four blocks over to Tracy's office. Strangely enough, Tracy wasn't in, either, but her secretary, Louise, was in a talkative mood, and since it was her coffee break, I took her down to the cafeteria on the fourth floor and treated her to a large Coke and several sugar-glazed donuts.

Louise was a buxom natural redhead with freckles on her plump arms and a wide, infectious grin. I'd known her since grade school, and I'd even taken her out a time or two our sophomore year. We'd never been any more than friends and she'd ended up married to her childhood sweetheart, Ryan Paris, who'd turned out to be a habitual flasher. By the time she'd discovered his secret out, they were already parents to three kids, so she tried to make the best of things, but one day Ryan had stepped out in front of a tourist bus to open his trench coat and had rather abruptly ended his career as a sex offender. Louise had collected a large sum from his life insurance policy, which she'd been diligent about keeping up, but eventually she gotten bored with staying at home, and when Tracy advertised for a secretary, she'd applied. Tracy, of course, knew Louise's history, but Louise was the only applicant who'd scored 130 words per minute on the typing test, and Tracy has an ever-abiding love of excellence. Louise had been hired on the spot.

Today she lined up her three sugar-coated donuts on a paper plate as she downed a syrupy Coke. She smiled at me with perfect white teeth set behind plump pink lips. "What can I do for you, Rick? I know you're not here just to watch me eat."

"That would be reason enough," I said, marveling at her capacity to put away junk food and still look as healthy and fresh as if she'd just stepped out of a cornfield. I knew for a fact that she already finished a pot of coffee a day; Tracy complained about it constantly.

"What can you tell me about Carl Bakersfield and his lovely bride?"

Louise looked out at me from under incongruously dark lashes. "I can tell you everything. I shouldn't tell you *anything.*"

"Pretty please?"

She laughed. "Ask me questions. I'll see if I can answer them without breaching lawyer-client confidentiality."

"You're not a lawyer."

"But I'm trying to get into law school, and I need Tracy's recommendation. It's not easy when you're pushing forty and female."

"Maybe you could just nod *yes* or *no.*"

179

"Try me."

"Okay. How long has Tracy been Carl's lawyer?"

"About four years. Since Carl and Perry came to La Jolla."

"Why did he pick Tracy?"

"Don't know that one. Yellow pages, maybe? Or maybe because Tracy represented Marilyn Cutter's dear old departed Dad?"

"Really? And when did Carl meet Marilyn Cutter?"

"Can't give you a date. I know she's the reason Carl came to San Diego."

"You're kidding!"

"Would I kid you?"

"She *brought* him out here?"

"Let's just say he met her before he came here, back east. Then when his parents died, I guess he had no reason to stay in Boston. Bad memories, maybe."

"Both his parents died at the same time?" Louise nodded. "Car wreck?" She shook her head. I frowned at her impatiently. "Do I have three guesses?"

She laughed. "Sorry." She took a huge bite of donut. I could hardly understand her through the crumbs when she spoke. "Fire."

"Fire? Did you say *fire?*"

"Yup. Their mansion caught fire. They were trapped inside."

"And where was Carl when this happened?"

"With Perry and Marilyn, dancing the night away. That's what they testified to at the inquest, at any rate."

I shook my head. "Curiouser and curiouser..."

Louise looked at her watch suddenly. She wiped donut from her plump pink lips. "Gotta go. Don't be a stranger, Rick. You're a lot more fun than your sister." She gave me an irrepressible grin and headed for the elevators. From behind, her extra ten pounds looked pretty good. She had a real redhead's pink glow that make everyone else around her look haggard. She'd make a great lawyer.

CHAPTER TWENTY-FOUR

Razor Moore was not the easiest ex-con

in the world to track down. I started with the phonebook and ended up putting out word on the street, with several frustrating steps in between. After three days of searching, I finally located Razor, and he agreed to meet me at my office--at midnight. I wasn't crazy about the idea of meeting an ex-con named Razor at such a vulnerable hour, so I took Charlie's earlier advice and went to get the .32 that Dad keeps in the wall safe at his house in Coronado.

Dad didn't look particularly happy to see me, but it probably had more to do with the late hour than with any true aversion to me on his part. He was in bed when I got there, wearing red long johns, and it had been so long since he'd opened the safe that he'd forgotten the combination. Finally he found a copy of it-- taped to the back of the framed Remington print that hid the safe. It didn't seem to me to be the best place to hide a combination, but I supposed that Dad's reasoning was that it was the last place any *serious* crook would *look*. It sounded so much like something Bree would say that I immediately stopped arguing, and I went to work opening the safe.

Inside it I found Dad's .32, which hadn't been shot since the day Dad bought it. Fortunately it was loaded, although why he bothered to keep a loaded gun in a wall safe was beyond me. I bid Dad goodbye. He was so irritable from being pulled out of bed that he didn't even ask me what I was going to do with the gun. As I was pulling out of the driveway, I understood why. Parked in the alley behind Dad's house was a familiar little white Alfa Romeo: *Mom's...*

* * *

Razor Moore arrived at my office promptly at midnight. I was sitting behind Rita's desk and I could hear him coming from two floors down, clomping his way up the wooden steps. Whatever he was, Razor certainly was no burglar. I pictured him as being the approximate size of a linebacker from the amount of noise he made, but when he came through the door, I realized that he couldn't have been much bigger than Bree was. His skin was the color of creamed coffee and his hair looked exactly like a rusty Brillo pad. He had huge, irregularly shaped freckles all over his face. His eyes were violet, like Elizabeth Taylor's. All in all he was a Technicolor dream, but nothing about him suggested a razor. Until he spoke.

He sounded like he'd been gargling razor blades.

He didn't smile when he saw me. He simply came forward and took a chair opposite my desk.

"You got the money?"

"Depends on what you're willing to tell me."

"This here's dangerous work, mister. Perry now, he'd slit my gizzard if he knew." He looked askance, as if Perry were already hiding behind the curtains, ready to do him in.

"Don't you read the papers, Razor? Perry Sinker's dead."

"Dead *my ass*," he growled, "ain't no more dead than you nor me." He looked me over. "Me, anyway..."

"You were his cellmate?"

"Among others."

"You mean Perry had other cellmates?"

He stared at me as if I were a dolt. "No, I mean *I* had other cellmates. Perry ain't been in the slammer but once. He's too smart to get caught again."

"Would you say he was suicidal?"

He rolled his eye. "Oh, brother!"

"What were *you* in for, Razor?"

"Arson."

I was astounded. "They put two arsonists in the same cell?"

Razor smirked, shutting his violet eyes. "Perry weren't much of an arsonist when I met him. Just a punk. Had no goals, but smart. I taught him everything he knows 'bout starting fires...he was nothing but a rank amateur when we met..." Again he opened his eyes, looked around furtively. "He'll *kill* me if he finds out I talked to you!"

"He's dead as far as anyone knows."

Razor turned those amazing purple eyes on me, focusing in. "You *stupid* or sumpin'? Perry Sinker ain't dead. Just wants folks to *think* he is. Perry Sinker'd crush your brain soon as *look* at you!"

I let that pass. "What did you teach him?"

"You got the money?"

"I've got it." I had two hundred dollars in cash in my wallet that I'd gotten out of the automatic teller on the way here. It was risky going to the automatic teller at night, but I had no choice. Besides, in my pocket was the .32. I could always brandish it in case of an emergency.

"Well, it was like this," Razor began. "I taught Perry to set a fuse. I like nitric acid, but Perry, he really took to potassium permanganate mixed up with glycerin. Can't detect that one so easy. See, Perry, he read books all the time, all the time! Damn cell was *filled* with his books! Crime books. Not true crime. Fiction! Got his ideas from them, he said. And once he got a little ambition, *brother!* That was it! The *sonovabitch*!" I winced as Razor's shrill voice hit a particular discordant pitch.

"Why do you say that? I thought you were his mentor."

Razor glared at me as if I'd called him a dirty word. "Ain't no mentor of no psychopath like that guy! Perry Sinker, he got no conscience. Split your skull open as soon as--"

"Okay, okay, so he wasn't a nice guy--"

"--*kill* me if he finds out I--"

"Did he ever ask you to help him with an arson job? Say, setting a mansion on fire?"

Razor grinned at me. "Hell no! I'm a *pyromaniac!* I set fires 'cause I get *off on it! I never* do it for *money*, that wouldn't be *right*," he said seriously.

"Did you ever associate with Perry after you two were released from prison?"

Razor was silent for a moment. "You promise not to tell? Because if he finds out he'll slit my--"

"I promise."

He looked out the window wistfully. "Once, 'bout a year ago, I saw him drivin' a fancy sports car with some dishy blonde beside him." He sighed. "You could tell he was livin' the *good* life. Ain't many of us get that chance..."

I handed him the two hundred dollars. "That's the truth."

He stood up and shoved the crumpled bills into his jeans pocket. "You promise me, you *see* him, you won't tell--"

"Razor, I won't. I swear on my daughter's life."

His face seemed to relax a bit. "Let me know if I can do anything else for you, mister. You're all right."

I gave him a smile. "I will, Razor, thanks." Razor charged out of my door and clattered noisily down the staircase. The plank floor rattled.

I looked at my watch. It was almost one a.m. A sudden rush of apprehension pushed against the base of my skull and I shivered. I fingered the .32 in my coat pocket.

Finally I went home to bed, but Razor's scratchy voice echoed shrilly in my dreams all night long...

CHAPTER TWENTY-FIVE

Bree moved her base of operation from our garage to the kitchen table.

"It's too dusty out there," she explained to me as she lined up her sculpting tools. "The clay was getting filthy."

Helen looked on, her lips pursed. "If you ask me, that's not *all* that's filthy! Fooling around with unholy--"

"It's not a real skull, Mother, it's a plaster cast! This is important work. I'm trying to identify a body."

Helen pursed her lips and left the room, her shoulders stiff. Bree shrugged, lifting the damp dishcloth from her creation. The head, if you could call it that, was fleshed out with realistic-looking clay muscles--all it needed now was skin, eyes, and hair. Bree was, in her own way, quite an artist. I was impressed.

"How much longer, do you think?"

She looked up at me. "A day, maybe two. I have to be extremely careful from here on in if I want to create an accurate likeness."

"No, I meant how much longer do you think your folks will be here?"

Bree sighed. "You got me. It's almost Thanksgiving, I assume they'll be staying for that. They haven't said anything about Christmas yet."

I patted her shoulder. "Not that I'm not enjoying sleeping on barbed wire, mind you. But I could use a little comfort and joy, if you catch my drift."

"I'd like to catch your drift," she whispered lasciviously.

Helen poked her head through the swinging door.

"I'm taking the baby to the park, Brendalee. I certainly don't want her around while you're working on that--abomination!"

Her head disappeared again and Bree looked up at me helplessly. "Come home early tonight, huh? I feel kind of green."

I kissed Bree's forehead gently. "Why don't you take it easy today? I'll get home as soon as I can. I promise."

* * *

Rita was standing on the sidewalk in front of our building as I pulled up. She was a bright vermilion sheath, and she tapped her high heels impatiently, as if she had been waiting for me a long time. I saw several men in business suits walk by her, staring, and one even began to approach her, but he changed his mind at the last minute and veered off reluctantly in another direction. When she caught sight of me, she pointed to the expensive gold watch on her wrist. I looked at my own watch; it was only ten. She caught my arm as I got out of the car and marched me up the steps toward our offices on the fourth floor.

"Guess who's here?"

"Buffalo Bob and Howdy Doody?"

"You're close. Your sister Tracy and Charlie Waxman. And they have a restraining order for you concerning the Bakersfield house. It seems Marilyn and Carl came home after a sailing trip to discover their guard dog bloodied and some items missing from the bedroom. For some reason they suspect you."

"I can't imagine why. I *love* dogs."

"Your prints, for one thing. Didn't you think to wear gloves?"

"...I forgot..."

Rita stopped on the second floor landing, staring at me with exasperation. "Look, Rick, it's only because Tracy and Charlie pleaded your case that you're not in the hoosegow already! Marilyn was determined to have you strung up by your--"

"Tracy stood up for me?" I asked, amazed.

"Apparently. But don't attribute any sisterly motives to her. I'm sure she's simply worried about her future career as district attorney."

I considered. "I don't suppose anyone mentioned Felton?"

Rita narrowed her eyes suspiciously. "What does Felton have to do with this?"

"Never mind," I answered hastily, starting up the steps again. "Let's just get this over with."

"My sentiments exactly," Rita growled.

"By the way," I said as we reached the fourth floor, where I could see Charlie's silhouette through the tinted office door. "How'd they know I'd be coming to the office?"

"Your mother-in-law informed them, I believe."

"That figures..."

* * *

"Dad told me you have his gun--" Tracy started viciously, "--and I don't know what you think you're going to do with it--"

"Well," I answered mildly, "I'm not going to shoot your client, if that's what you're afraid of!"

"Can't you two be in the same room without all this hostility?" Charlie pleaded.

"No!" we answered in unison, glaring at each other.

Charlie sighed, handing me a writ. "It says you have to stay away from both the property and the persons of Mr. and Mrs. Carl Bakers--"

"I know what it says..." I said impatiently, snatching the paper and stuffing it into my pocket. "So? Anything else? Want to spank my hands, Tracy?"

Tracy gave me the coldest look she would allow herself, turned on her heel, and stomped out.

Charlie watched her go, then turned back to me and clicked his tongue. "She's not really that bad, Rick..."

"What criteria are you using to judge her, Charlie? The length of her skirt?"

"She's a good lawyer. She's looking out for her clients' interests!"

"Her clients are conniving criminals!"

Charlie looked interested suddenly. "You have proof of that?"

I stood up and pushed him gently into a chair. "Did you know both of Carl Bakersfield's parents died in a deliberately-set fire right before he migrated from Boston to California?"

"So?"

"So Perry Sinker was a convicted *arsonist.* And Carl was an only child. He inherited everything, which was quite a lot. I even found out that there's a standing reward of fifty thousand dollars leading to the arrest of anyone involved in the death of the Bakersfields."

"Did Carl put it up?"

"Are you kidding? Mrs. Bakersfield's sister did. She hates Carl, apparently. Told Rita on the phone that it's Carl's fault that her sister is dead."

"Wasn't Carl investigated at the time of the fire?"

I turned away reluctantly. "Prints didn't match."

Charlie raised an eyebrow. "Maybe he had the good sense to wear *gloves.* Which was more than I can say for you..."

I turned back to Charlie, infuriated. "Don't act dumb with me, Charlie Waxman, I know you too well! You're just as suspicious as I am!"

Charlie sat back in the chair, pulling his pipe out of his breast pocket. "You've been a busy boy...what else have you found out?"

I eyed him dubiously. "I'm not sure I'm willing to share information when you've got such strong interest in the enemy camp."

Charlie snorted. "Tracy? Forget it. She's too concerned with her future to risk it on a lowbrow *schmo* like me."

I waited a moment while Charlie attempted futilely to light his pipe.

He looked up at me. "Well?"

"Did you know that Marilyn knew Carl and Perry in Boston before Carl's parents died? Did you know that Perry Sinker was in love with Marilyn? Did you know that the shoes Perry Sinker was wearing when he supposedly jumped off the Coronado Bridge were found in Marilyn's closet at Carl's house--"

"Whoa! Wait a minute! Slow down!" Charlie puffed madly at his unlit pipe. "Is there a theory in all this, or are you just making lists?"

I rubbed my head. "I'm not sure. Something tells me that the three of them were involved with Carl's parents' deaths, but I couldn't say just how. And I know Carl has those Zapata twins stowed away somewhere because they saw something they shouldn't have, but I don't know *what*. I have a strong feeling that Perry Sinker's still alive, but I don't know where he is. And I know that Marilyn's hiding something, but I don't know what it is."

Charlie stared at me. "What *do* you know, exactly?"

"I'm not sure..."

"Great. That's where we started."

"Look, you're the cop on the case! Can't you contribute something?"

"Well..." Charlie reached into his pocket and pulled out his matches. "I *do* know that Marilyn's father's will is being read this afternoon--"

"That's perfect!"

"--but *you're* not allowed to come within fifty feet of her, remember? I'm the one who *signed* that restraining order!"

I considered for a moment. "It says I can't be within fifty feet of them?"

"Right."

"Bodily?"

"How else?"

* * *

I caught Tracy's secretary, Louise, on her lunch break. Now Louise was a woman with a sense of humor. She had no qualms whatsoever about putting the transmitter Felton had bought second-hand for me right next to her intercom system.

"Tracy will think it's a new piece of computer equipment," she chuckled. I knew from experience that Tracy had about as much computer aptitude as I did.

189

At three o'clock Rita, Felton and I gathered in my office for the broadcast. We ended up waiting forty-five minutes until all the parties involved finally arrived. It seemed Marilyn was having a facial that had run overtime. The signal from the transmitter was dim, but clear. I could distinguish Tracy's voice, along with Marilyn's, and an older female voice I took to be Yvonne Cutter, Marilyn's mother. There were two male voices I didn't recognize, but I assumed they were Marilyn's brothers.

After the niceties, Tracy began the preliminaries with a lot of legal rigmarole that didn't amount to much, except to establish the fact that Sebastian Cutter was dead and that Tracy's law firm was the legal executor of his will, which Tracy would proceed to read to the heirs.

I detected a hint of nervousness to Tracy's voice that I'd never heard before. Rita and Felton must have noticed it too--we all began to tense, straining toward the receiver.

First came the part establishing the fact that Clifford Sebastian Cutter was of sound mind and body. After that came the part we were all waiting for: the bequests.

As expected, Mrs. Cutter received the largest bequest: a third of the estate, to be kept in trust and doled out as needed. After having seen Mrs. Cutter and her bodice-rippers, I felt Sebastian had made a wise decision. Next the will left specific sums to various charities, including a large amount earmarked for the Republican Party, to which he credited the soundness of the economy. I heard Louise guffaw at that remark. Next came his bequests to his three children. Rita, Felton and I held our breaths.

To his oldest son, Nelson, he bequeathed fifteen million dollars to use wholly at his discretion. Nelson also got the family mansion, on the terms that he house his mother for the remainder of her life.

To his younger son, Dwight, he bequeathed ten million dollars and his vacation home in Aruba.

When Tracy got to the part about his bequest to Marilyn, she began to choke. From the sounds we heard, we gathered that someone got her a glass of water. After a few moments and some swallowing noises, Tracy continued to read, her voice quavering a full octave higher than usual.

"...and to my daughter, Marilyn, I bequeath my yacht, *The Night Cry*, and the sum of four hundred and seventy-two dollars, to be used specifically to have her hull scraped..." Tracy paused uncertainly. "I think he means the *yacht's* hull..."

Total silence.

Then Marilyn's voice. "Go on!"

"That's all." Tracy said weakly.

Rita and I looked at each other. There was silence for another moment, then, abruptly, the ring of breaking glass.

"Now Marilyn--"

"SHUT UP YOU SONOVABITCH!"

Another crash. "Marilyn, darling, don't call your brother--"

"HOW COULD HE! HOW COULD HE!"

I heard a sound that indicated to me that my sister's fancy smoked glass desk might be a thing of the past.

"Call the doctor! She needs a tranquillizer!"

"YOU CHEATING--"

"Clear the room!"

"Louise, call 911!"

Louise's voice, calm and amused as always, came over the receiver. "Sorry, Rick, we got a little emergency. Mad dog. Call you later." She chuckled and pulled the plug.

For a moment of dumbfounded silence we just sat and stared at the receiver. Then Rita turned to me. "Just one question. Where was hubby Carl today?"

I frowned. "I don't know. Maybe he was there and just wasn't saying anything."

Felton whistled. "What a broad! Whew! Imagine what she's like in a clinch!"

Rita stood up. "I've got to get back to work. If you two figure anything out, let me know."

She trotted back into the outer office, where Wanda was brushing her shining black hair. When Rita opened the door between us, Wanda caught a glimpse of me and winked. I frowned at her and turned to Felton.

"How come you didn't leave any fingerprints at the Bakersfield place?"

Felton grinned. "Surgical gloves. Latex. Didn't you notice?"

"You mean that nasty little dog ripped through surgical gloves?"

"Shredded them. Probably would have been worse if I hadn't been wearing them. So what do you think?"

I shrugged. "I think we'll find the truth when we find Perry Sinker."

Felton nodded. "Amen, brother!"

CHAPTER TWENTY-SIX

Bree was having a bad night. She tossed and turned and kept getting up to go to the bathroom. She'd always been the proverbial picture of health and I was definitely worried about her. She still looked pale in the morning, but she couldn't pin it down to any one malady.

"Maybe you're allergic to something in that clay," I offered.

She shook her head. "Same brand I used before." She saw the worried look on my face and smiled slightly. "I'm just a little stressed out. If I don't start feeling better soon, I'll go see Dr. James. She'll probably just tell me to slow it down a little."

"Probably." At least Bree's doctor wasn't an octogenarian like our family doctor, but the whole idea of Bree needing a doctor at all appalled me. "Are you sure you don't want me to stay home with you today?"

"Are you kidding?" She rolled her eyes. "I have my Mommy. What more could I possibly need?"

* * *

The morgue never gets any better, no matter how many times you go there. Bree and I had ended up at the morgue on our very first date, but somehow that fact does not lend it any sentimental value for me. I didn't like it then and I don't like it now.

"Recognize him?" Granger Spoon pulled back the white sheet unceremoniously. I stared down at huge brown freckles and rusty Brillo hair.

"Razor Moore." The violet eyes were shut permanently and the rasping voice stilled--someone had slit his throat.

Granger covered the corpse in its drawer and slid it back into the refrigerated wall. He plopped down into his chair, pulled the rubber band from his ponytail, and shook his gray hair loose. "How's Bree doing with the skull?"

"She's not feeling too well right now."

He looked concerned. "I'll give her a call."

Charlie, who had been leaning against the far wall silently, pointed a finger at me and said, "My office. *Now.*" He walked out of the door.

Granger raised his brows. "*Uh-oh.* You been a naughty boy?"

"How long's Razor been dead?"

Granger considered. "I'd say twenty-four hours, more or less. Probably died after midnight on Tuesday morning. He was tucked into an alley down in the Gas Lamp. Isn't your office over there, Rick?"

Razor's scratchy voice rang in my ears:

"He'll kill me if he finds out I talked to you!"

* * *

"Perry Sinker did it!" I knew I was waving my arms around like a madman, but I couldn't seem to control myself. "You should have seen poor Razor, he was terrified of the guy!"

For once Charlie looked as upset as I felt. He stood stiffly, staring at the various citations he had framed and hung on his office wall.

"You were the last one to see him alive, Rick..."

"I know! How do you think that makes me feel?"

"I don't know. How did it make you feel when you broke into Carl Bakersfield's mansion?"

Now I was confused. "What are you getting at?"

Charlie turned to me. "I keep telling you to back off of this case, and every time I turn around, something worse has happened and you're right in the middle of it! Rick, you're my best friend in the world, and you know I'd do anything for Bree and Margaret, but I'm telling you that if your name comes up one more time in this office in connection with this case, I'll have you arrested!"

"Are you serious?"

"I'm dead serious! You'd better stick to divorces, pal, you're in way over your head!"

I looked at him. He avoided my eyes. I grabbed his arm. "You know something you're not telling me!"

"Marilyn Bakersfield's father disinherited her," he said slowly.

"Oh, that," I sneered, my disappointment showing. "Tell me something I don't already know."

Charlie whirled. "How the hell do you know about that? You're barred from stepping--"

"Look, word gets round," I answered hastily.

"Well, it better not get around *you* any more!" Charlie shouted. "I mean it, Rick! No more involvement in this! You understand? I'm pulling rank on you before you get yourself hurt!"

"Like Razor Moore?"

"You can't get any deader than that."

"In other words, you admit that there might be something to all this."

Charlie rubbed his jaw. "If there is, the police department will handle it. Butt out, Rick, or you'll end up on somebody's hit list."

He slumped into the chair behind his desk. I'd never seen Charlie look so defeated.

"All right," I said slowly. "I'll back off. This isn't my case anyway."

Charlie looked up, saw that I meant it, and brightened considerable. It wasn't until that point that I believed he was genuinely worried that I might get myself killed. He got up and threw his arm around my shoulder.

"That's more like it! And I don't want you to worry. I'm putting a couple of my best detectives on the Razor Moore killing. If Perry Sinker's alive, we'll find him!"

"If he *stays* alive..."

Charlie looked flummoxed. "What do you mean?"

I smiled. "Nothing. I just hope Perry's the worst thing we have to contend with..."

Charlie frowned. "Not *we*, Rick. Me. You're out of this."

"Whatever you say, Chief..."

* * *

I decided to drop by my office and check up on things on my way home. I couldn't stop thinking about poor Razor, who'd probably still be alive if I hadn't dug him out of the woodwork. I had the sense of a single mind behind all this, someone who had schemed for years and whose carefully-wrought plan was unraveling before his eyes. I've known people like that before, people who figure their lives out in five-year blocks, but they generally aren't criminals. In fact, my sister Tracy is one of them. She's known since grade school what she wanted, and she's gone after it with a bulldog tenacity that alarmed my parents. I don't think it had ever occurred to her even once that what she wanted was not necessarily best for those nearest and dearest to her. Her quest for the office of District Attorney was a prime example. No doubt the reason Dad had ended up in the hospital was Tracy's insistence on this plan of hers to be a political power in San Diego. For all we knew, she might have her eye on the presidency, which was a horrifying thought.

I was a block away from my office when my tire blew with a tremendous bang. It made me furious, because I'd just replaced the two front tires, and the back ones weren't more than a year old. I was downtown and there was nowhere to pull over, so I swerved the car into the nearest alleyway and got out to have a look. The front left tire was as flat as warm beer. There was a huge hole in it, as if someone had blown it up like a balloon until it had burst. I ducked down for a closer look, swearing, because I knew that I'd lost the warranty papers on that tire, and as I stood up again, I heard another deafening bang, this one uncomfortably close to my right ear. At the same time the bricks directly behind my head seemed to explode, sending showers of red clay splinters into my hair.

The third bullet struck my back car window seconds later. The glass cracked like ice, but it didn't fall out. Safety glass. Great invention.

I hit the dirt with my hands over my head, waiting for the final shot, the shot that would splatter my blood across the pavement. I could hear footsteps approaching slowly from the street. Where the hell was my *gun*? I remembered setting it on the end table last night, but when I'd gotten up this morning I'd forgotten all about it. Was it still sitting there, waiting for Margaret's tiny hands to accidentally trip the trigger?

In a last ditch attempt to save myself, I stuck my hands deep into my coat pockets. My fingers collided with steel. Good old Bree! I yanked the gun out as the footsteps stopped right beside me, and flipping not-too-gracefully onto my back, I pointed the barrel straight up and growled, "If you come any closer I'll blow your brains out!"

A familiar voice chuckled, "Blow my brains out? Who are you supposed to be, Dirty Harry?"

A huge rough hand reached down and swiped the gun away, while another pulled me to my feet. "You okay, Mr. Matthews?" Vern Sheffield, the porno show owner from across the street, stood there squinting at me in the dim light, his arsenal at the ready. "Somebody after you? I heard shots! You hit?"

"I don't think so. Did you see anybody?"

Vern grinned. "Nope. Just you lyin' on your face in the muck. That ain't no way to defend yourself." I brushed myself off, my neck reddening. "You need a bodyguard? My son Ralph, he's available--"

"Thanks, Vern, I'm fine..."

Vern scowled at me. "I'm not so sure. Guy got his throat slit right in this alley the other night. Best take precautions." He walked me down the block and up to my office. "You did me a good turn, Mr. Matthews, finding Mom like that for me. Let me help you out. I'll send Ralph over to your house, he never sleeps!"

I had had occasion to meet Ralph while Dad and I were in Vern's employ, and I wasn't anxious to have him in my living room. He was a polite twenty-five year old, but he looked a little like a battered refrigerator and he'd spent too much time in street fights getting his brain rattled to have much judgment left. The idea of him near my family with firearms didn't appeal to me.

Nevertheless, I was grateful that Vern had come along when he did. Otherwise I would have ended up as shattered as that window. It helps to have friends in the Gas Lamp.

* * *

Bree came to pick me up in her new Mustang. Mine was hauled away by the city for illegally obstructing an alleyway before I had time to dial AAA. I called the Traffic Control Department instead, but nobody seemed to be able to locate my car. That was the last straw in an already-maddening day. Bree wasn't happy to discover that someone was gunning for me. In fact, she called Charlie and burned up his line for half an hour, using language I didn't even know she knew. After she hung up, she came into the living room and sat down beside me on the couch.

"Perry's back, isn't he?"

I nodded. "I guess I know too much. So to speak."

"Maybe we should take a vacation..."

I smiled at her worried face. "What do you have in mind?"

"Nova Scotia?"

"Too cold."

"Probably no colder than here." She hugged herself, shivering. "And a lot friendlier."

"We can't run away from this, Bree."

She looked at me critically. "Why not?"

She had a point. I was trying to think of an answer when Margaret staggered in and climbed onto my lap. She was dressed in a fleecy pink sleeper, and she dragged her scarlet silky inexorably behind her. Her soft baby cheek grazed my shoulder and she fell asleep instantly. I suddenly realized that Helen and Hugo were nowhere to be seen.

"Where're your folks?"

"They rented a car and went to spend a free night at the Lawrence Welk Retirement Village in Escondido."

"A free night? You don't mean they're actually considering--"

Bree shrugged. "Who knows what they're considering. They're aliens. We can't comprehend their thought processes."

Now I understood the not-so-subtle hints Helen had been dropping for the last week, comments about Margaret needing her grandparents close by. I thought she was lobbying for us to move back to the Midwest.

"Can they afford to live in California?"

"I suppose so. Their house is paid off. It's worth five times what they paid for it thirty years ago. They could probably afford a condo."

We looked at each other a little desperately.

"Maybe I'll get shot," I said.

"You'd better not," Bree answered darkly. "They'd make me move in with them. Lester would have to go back to the pound."

We stared morosely into the gloom.

Abruptly the doorbell began ringing. Bree jumped. "Let's not answer it!"

"Don't be silly, Bree." In the backyard I could hear Lester start to yowl. Soon he'd wake up the whole neighborhood. I handed Margaret to Bree.

"But someone's trying to kill you!" she pleaded.

I hesitated, considering whether to let Lester into the house, just in case. The doorbell quit ringing and I heard a voice. *"Rick! Open up! It's an emergency!"*

I flung open the front door. Felton stood there in a state of panic.

I frowned. "Felton, what the hell--"

"Come on, Rick, we got to go!"

Margaret woke in Bree's arms and started to cry. "Now look, you woke up the baby--"

He grabbed my arm. "Get the lead out, Rick! *We gotta go!* There's a three-alarm fire at the Bakersfield mansion! Looks like arson!"

Bree went white. For a moment I thought she would faint, but she stood up, swaying, the baby clinging to her. "Bree? You okay?"

She looked at me resolutely, regaining her color, and set her jaw. With Bree it's never over till it's over. Before I could say get in another word, she'd grabbed her backpack, Margaret firmly in tow. She smiled stiffly. "Well? What are we waiting for?"

CHAPTER TWENTY-SEVEN

The Bakersfield mansion was burning

with a rage usually reserved for forest fires. Smoke billowed a hundred feet into the sky, giving the impression from the freeway that a small nuclear bomb had been dropped in the middle of La Jolla. Close up, it was another story. The night was freezing, but for once I was too warm. Five fire trucks crowded the cul-de-sac, trying to drench what was once the most expensive house on the block. Soon it would be blackened rubble.

Marilyn Cutter stood in a puddle of water on her newly sodded front lawn, screaming at the top of her lungs, her whole body straining toward the fire. She was being restrained by four yellow-slickered firemen, who had to struggle to keep a grip on her. Her ice-blue negligee was streaked with soot and her ivory hair, for once, hung limply around her ears. Carl was nowhere in sight. I was just wondering what had happened to Marilyn's little brown dachshund when I heard a low snarl at my feet.

Felton looked down and I saw him turn pale. "*Oh no...*" he cried faintly, stepping back. Bree, still balancing Margaret in her arms, saw the tiny terror and immediately stamped her foot sharply against the soggy grass. "*Beat it!*" she barked in a deep, authoritative voice. The little beast looked up at her uncertainly, then turned slowly and trotted back to Marilyn's side, glancing over its shoulder now and then at this new threat to its dominance.

Abruptly the second floor of the mansion exploded and the whole structure seemed to collapse upon itself. Following suit, Marilyn screamed "*CARL!*" and fainted dead away. The four firemen tried to pick her up and place her on a stretcher, but her faithful little dog, attempting to protect her, sunk his fangs into the nearest one. There was a fracas in which the firemen were getting the worst of it, until one of them lit upon the idea of turning the hose on the hound. They hit on its side with one stinging blast of cold, hard water, and it fled, yelping with terror. Immediately the paramedics slid Marilyn into a waiting ambulance and drove off.

The little dachshund, now bereft of adversaries, slunk off to sulk in the bushes. It wasn't until the fire had begun finally to burn itself out that I noticed Charlie. He was standing about ten feet away from us, gazing at the flames, his suit soaked, a vicious red scratch evident on his cheek.

He looked over and saw me and his face stiffened, but he didn't say anything. He turned away and pretended I wasn't there. Bree raised an eyebrow, but decided that enough was enough for one night. She nudged Felton and we all climbed into the Bobsled from Hell. It'd been a long day.

* * *

I have to admit that I was surprised when Charlie called me the next morning. He asked me to meet him at the Gourmet Hamburger in Mission Valley, across from the shopping center. This was a favorite place of Charlie's. There were no waitresses in mini-skirts, but each table had its own red telephone so you could phone in your order, and the hamburgers were varied and delicious. It was also just a stone's throw from our house in Kensington. I thought maybe he was planning on lecturing me about being at the fire the night before. I was wrong.

"This is the way it is," he started, spreading his huge beefy hands on the table before him. He'd already ordered his burger, and mine too, but they weren't ready yet. "We found Carl Bakersfield's remains in the wreckage of the mansion this morning. He was burned beyond recognition, but his wedding

202

ring was still intact, and we're sending to Boston for his medical and dental records just to confirm."

"How's Marilyn taking it?"

He touched his raked cheek gingerly. "Better than last night. She's sedated. She's staying at her mother's house right now." He stared expectantly at me.

"So?" I said, slightly irritated at his change in demeanor.

"Marilyn saw Perry Sinker."

"What?"

"Right before the fire. She says she was walking Ferdinand--"

"Ferdinand? You mean that vicious little hot dog of hers?"

"--and when she came in and turned to lock up, she could see Perry through the front window, lurking in the bushes."

"Lurking? Was that her word?"

"Wait a minute--I have her deposition in my pocket." He reached into his inner coat pocket just as our burgers arrived. For a moment I could see the struggle in his eyes as he tried to decide whether his hamburger or Marilyn's deposition had priority, but he finally pushed the sandwich aside and pulled out a stapled set of typed papers.

"Jan Merkle took this statement from Marilyn Cutter while when she was still in the hospital."

"Was she hurt?"

Charlie shrugged. "Just a little smoke inhalation..." He ran his finger down the lines of type. "*Here it is...'I could see Perry lurking in the bushes. He was carrying a device of some kind.'*" Charlie looked at me.

I frowned. "A device? What does that mean?"

"I guess she meant a suspicious-looking package." He looked back down at the deposition and read again. "'*I saw him go around to the back of the house. I don't think he saw me. I was just about to go upstairs and tell Carl when there was an explosion and the house was on fire. I screamed for Carl and tried to make up the stairs, but the fire spread so fast I barely had time to pick up Ferdinand and get out of the door...'*"

Charlie put the deposition down, unable to resist his burger any longer.

"What do you think?" he mumbled between bites.

"What difference does it make *what* I think?" I answered, annoyed. "You told me yesterday to keep the hell away from this."

Charlie looked hurt. "I was just trying to protect you. But now somebody's shooting at you, Rick, and with Carl Bakersfield dead, it looks like you might just have been right about Perry."

I watched him eat for a moment, my appetite strangely subdued. Usually I was a sucker for any kind of red meat, but just now I could only concentrate on one thing at a time. Like staying alive. It was pretty likely that Perry wasn't going to stop at Carl and Razor Moore--at the rate he was going, he was likely to wipe out the entire population of San Diego before he was through.

"Did you find the device?"

Charlie nodded. "Part of it. Lab's analyzing it now." He wolfed the rest of his hamburger and washed it down with a generous gulp of Coke. "We found something else, Rick."

"Yeah?"

"It seemed to be the remnants of a chemistry set. You know, the kind you get when you're a kid."

"Maybe *you* did. My father got *me* a Lionel Train. I hated chemistry."

"The Zapata twins didn't..."

I looked up sharply. Charlie continued to eye me expectantly. "So? Are you saying you think the twins made the bomb that blew up the house?"

"Don't be ridiculous! But I am saying that there's evidence that they've been there recently."

I jumped up from the table. "Charlie, damnit, I could wring your neck! Why do you think I wanted a search warrant? How the hell am I going to explain it to Delores Zapata if her precious boys died in that fire?"

"Calm down. They didn't. There were no other remains besides Carl's." I sat back down, picking at my French fries. Charlie and I stared at each other for a moment, each contemplating the jigsaw puzzle laid out before us.

"Okay, let's be logical about this," I said logically. "Take it one step at a time...." Charlie smiled patiently. "First: who stood to gain by Perry Sinker's suicide?"

"Monetarily?"

"Perry was as broke as I am, so there had to be some other reason."

Charlie leaned back expansively, picking his teeth with an automatic teller card he'd pulled from his wallet.

"Well, Felton says the only two motives for any crime are money or sex." He laughed.

"Felton's an idiot!" I said sourly. "Unless...wait a minute. Maybe it *was* sex! Carl married Marilyn so Perry could have her, but maybe Carl really wanted her for himself! Or maybe Marilyn wanted Carl!"

"You seem to be forgetting something. Your friend Felton saw Perry throw himself over the edge of the bridge. Besides, we know Perry isn't dead now. Marilyn saw him just last night!"

I slumped back in my seat, staring at my sandwich. Nothing made any sense. My stomach was beginning to hurt. I wondered if peptic ulcers could be hereditary.

"Why don't you make it simple for everybody, Charlie, and put out an all-points bulletin on Perry Sinker?"

"Well, we've got a little problem with that...the only picture we have of Perry Sinker is his mug shot, and he's wearing a full-scale beard and hair to his shoulders. I doubt if anyone will recognize him from that."

"What about Marilyn?"

"She's unconscious. Her doctor has her completely sedated."

I had a sudden thought. "Tracy knew Perry! She could give the police artist a description!"

"That's a great idea, Rick! You ask her."

"Me!"

"You're her brother--"

"--and you're the officer on the case! Don't be such a wimp!" Charlie looked downhearted. I took pity on him.

"We'll go to her office together. It'll be two against one."

Charlie paid the bill, rubbing the back of his neck briskly. "When this is over with I'm going to fly to Hawaii and spend a week and do nothing but sit in the water and play with the crabs..."

I snorted. "Sure! With all those bikinis around?"

Charlie sighed softly. "No...Bree was right...I'm a middle-aged man. Chasing skirts gets me nothing but trouble. Then I find a woman I can really fall in love with and—*pow!* She *dumps* me!"

I looked at Charlie incredulously. "You can't mean Tracy!"

He nodded miserably. I contemplated him with awe. He suddenly seemed like the bravest person I knew. A romantic encounter with Tracy had to be akin to swimming in a shark tank at feeding time.

"Cheer up, Charlie. Look at it this way. After Bree and Tracy, the rest of your life should be a cinch!" He smiled slightly, but his heart wasn't in it.

CHAPTER TWENTY-EIGHT

Louise was not at her desk in the reception room of Tracy's office when Charlie and I arrived, so we decided to just barge right in. Unfortunately for everyone concerned, we barged in at the wrong moment. Tracy was in her office, all right, engaged in what could only be described as a tense conversation with her steely-eyed husband Maynard.

They both looked up at the same time as we came in. Tracy saw Charlie and grimaced. Maynard's steely eyes grew steelier. I tried to smile.

"Hiya, Trace!"

"Get out of here, Rick!" she hissed through clenched teeth, but by then it was too late. Maynard crossed the white rug in two long strides and landed a punch on Charlie's jaw that knocked him sideways over the couch.

"Maynard!" Tracy screamed, rushing over to Charlie and kneeling down before him. Maynard stared at her coldly, then, without uttering a single word to any of us, exited.

I walked over to Tracy, who by this time was cradling Charlie's head in her lap.

"I guess you told him, huh?"

"No, I did *not* tell him! Do you think I'm an idiot?"

"Is that a rhetorical question?"

"Louise told him!" she hissed, her eyes filling with tears. One of them dropped down and hit Charlie right on the nose. He had been lying there in a stupor, but the tear seemed to rouse him and he opened his eyes.

"Where is Louise?" I asked Tracy.

"I fired her, of course!" Charlie sat up suddenly and Tracy jumped out of his way. When he looked at her, it was a look of abject sorrow.

"I'm so sorry, Tracy! I didn't mean--"

Tracy sat down abruptly on her couch, crossing her legs and fishing in her pocket for a cigarette. She lit up and looked at the two of us sternly.

"It's my own damn fault! I can't blame you, Charlie, you're a sentimental fool. I'm the one who knew better..."

She sat staring at the wall for a moment, smoking, then suddenly she mashed out the cigarette in the crystal-cut glass ashtray in front of her. "Well, that's that."

She looked up at us, as if she'd cheerfully resigned herself to her fate, and her smile was almost friendly.

"Okay, boys. What can I do for you?"

* * *

When I called Bree from Tracy's office there was no answer, not even the familiar buzz of the answering machine. I thought maybe she'd gone to see her doctor, but when I phoned the clinic, no one had heard from her. I tried Jane's house. Jane wasn't home. I started to worry.

"I can't find Bree...She isn't at home, and I've got her car! Where could she have gotten to?"

Charlie was lying on Tracy's white designer couch, trying to decide whether Maynard had broken his jaw or had simply dislodged a tooth. "Bree can take care of herself, Rick," said Tracy, "--as we both well know!"

"Tracy," Charlie said gently, "someone shot at Rick yesterday. Four times."

Tracy frowned. "I don't believe you!"

"Do you believe that Carl Bakersfield burned to death in his mansion last night?" I asked nastily.

Tracy turned ashen. "Oh my God..."

"Don't you read the papers?"

She shook her head. "Maynard and I were fighting--"

I turned to Charlie. "Look, I've got to get home!" I started out the door, suddenly feeling panicky. "Hurry up!"

Charlie turned to Tracy and shrugged, but she grabbed her coat and hurried after us. "I'll go with you!"

We went downstairs and piled into Charlie's squad car, which was illegally parked in a bus zone. Charlie flipped on the lights and the siren and we roared the distance between downtown and Kensington in seven minutes flat. I sat in the front and Tracy in the back, leaning on her elbows between the two of us.

"Just what was so important that you two had to burst into my office and wreck my marriage?" she managed to shout over the scream of the siren.

"We need a description of Perry Sinker," I shouted back. "Marilyn says she saw him last night lurking in her bushes just before the house caught on fire."

Tracy snorted. "I'll just bet he was lurking in her bushes! Why don't you get a description from her?"

"She's unconscious. Brokenhearted over losing her hubby, no doubt," I added.

"She fired me, you know," Tracy said matter-of-factly.

I looked at her, shocked. "Marilyn fired you? Why?"

"She blames me because her father changed his will before he died. Of course, he had me send her a copy at the time. How was I supposed to know?"

"Know what?"

Tracy smiled slightly. "Marilyn's as dyslexic as Cher. She can't even read a stop sign! Apparently she was totally unaware of the fact that her father intended to cut her off. He was smart enough to leave her his boat and a pittance, so she really has no grounds to contest the will."

"So now Marilyn's penniless?" Charlie asked.

Tracy sat for a moment without answering. "Well, she *was*," she said finally, "before Carl died in that fire..."

We looked at each other. The car pulled up in front of my house and I jumped out and headed for the door at full speed, yanking my key out of my pocket and jamming it into the lock.

Lester set up a yowl in the backyard that would wake the dead. I fiddled with the key until it turned, but before I could push open the door open, it was yanked away from me and I fell inward onto my face.

I looked up. Staring down at me, greatly puzzled, was Wanda, my little Mexican secretary, balancing Margaret on one of her round hips. When she saw it was me, she grinned with delight.

"Daddy!" Margaret squealed.

"Senor Matthews! *Como esta*?" I got to my feet, searching the room. "Bree!" I shouted. Tracy and Charlie came in through the door behind me. Charlie smiled at Wanda, who smiled back shyly. I ran to the kitchen. Bree was gone. On the table in the dining room, covered with a damp dishcloth, was the skull Bree had been working on. Behind it, on her computer screen, I could make out several paragraphs of her article for *The Reader*.

I accosted Wanda. "Where'd Bree go?" She looked at me blankly. "Bree! My wife!"

"*Esposa*," Charlie offered helpfully.

"Wanda! *Donde esta mi esposa*?" I said.

Her eyes lit up. "Ah. *No esta aqui*."

"I *know* she's not here!" I shouted, exasperated. "I want to know where she *is*!"

Wanda's lip came out in a little pout. She didn't like being shouted at. I turned to Margaret.

"Miss Button?" Margaret grinned at me. "Do you know where Mommy went?" She nodded her head solemnly. "Where did she go, honey? Did she go with Grandma and Grandpa?"

Margaret shook her strawberry curls. "Did she go with Aunt Janie?" Again she shook her head. "With Aunt Rita?"

"No. With the *lady*."

I frowned. "Lady? What lady?"

"With white hair. The *smell-good* lady."

Behind me Tracy let out an ear-splitting scream. Charlie reached for his shoulder holster and I grabbed the gun out of my pocket and whirled to see that Tracy had pulled the cloth from the skull and was staring at the clay face in horror.

I pocketed the automatic. "It's just *clay,* Tracy," I said in disgust, "don't be so squeamish."

Her eyes were riveted to the skull. "It's Perry Sinker!" she cried.

Charlie took her shoulders gently. "It can't be. The coroner already ruled that the skull didn't—"

Tracy turned on him furiously. "That's Perry Sinker, I tell you! I knew the man for three years! Do you think I'm an--"

"Tracy, Marilyn just saw Perry Sinker last night outside her window!" I interrupted.

"*She* says! And *I* say that that face belongs to the man I knew as Perry Sinker!"

The three of us stood staring at the clay face: the blonde hair, the deep-set blue glass eyes.

Abruptly Charlie's beeper went off. He looked at me, let out a deep sigh, and went back into the living room to dial his office.

Tracy stood staring at the face. I sat down heavily on the fold-out couch. Wanda, still balancing Margaret on her hip, came and sat down beside me, fluttering her thick black lashes, obviously undeterred by the fact that I was a family man.

A few minutes later Charlie came back into the kitchen. The look on his face was enough to bring me to my feet.

"What is it, Charlie?"

He cleared his throat. "That was Granger Spoon, the coroner," he said slowly, as if he were choosing his words very carefully. "He's been working on the identification of the remains that were found in the Bakersfield mansion." He cleared his throat again. Tracy gave him an impatient look. "So? What did he find out?"

"He sent to Boston for Carl Bakersfield's records. He found out that Carl had un-erupted wisdom teeth--and a congenitally missing little finger."

I sat back, stunned, feeling as if I'd been hit with a baseball bat. Tracy still didn't get it. "So? What's the rest of it?"

Charlie fixed her with his eyes. "The remains found at the Bakersfield mansion show that the victim died from a blow to the skull with a sharp object, *not* from smoke inhalation. It was murder."

Tracy narrowed her eyes skeptically. "You're trying to tell me that someone murdered Carl Bakersfield with an axe?"

Charlie shook his head. "Not Carl. Perry. It was Perry Sinker's body we found in the fire." He turned and pointed dramatically to the clay-covered skull.

"That," he said, "is the real Carl Bakersfield..."

CHAPTER TWENTY-NINE

Tracy let it sink in. "Carl and Perry switched identities? *Why?*"

"Perry's idea, after he burnt down Carl's parents?"

Tracy shook her head furiously. "I didn't know anything about this! I'm sure Marilyn's parents didn't either. The only one who could have known about this was--"

Good-smell lady. White haired lady. I looked up at Tracy helplessly. "Oh God. Bree's with Marilyn!"

Charlie shook his head. "She can't be. Marilyn's sedated. Besides, I left her with a twenty-four hour guard."

Tracy turned to him. "Charlie. Call."

Charlie escaped again to the living room. Tracy came over to me and put her hand on mine. It was the first nonviolent physical contact we'd had in twenty-five years. Wanda shot her a jealous look. She turned on her heel and stalked out of the room with the baby.

"Don't worry," Tracy murmured softly. "Bree's fine. I'm sure of it."

"I'm not," I said bluntly. Charlie returned, looking chagrined.

"Marilyn left her mother's house about two hours ago. Her mother says she was going for a sail, but she's about half-cracked anyway. I called the office and alerted them to pick Marilyn up. And Bree too, if they're together."

I looked at him. "Great. Just great. What am I supposed to do now, sit here and rot while my wife--"

"Let's put out a dragnet!" interrupted Tracy. "How far could they have gone? Why don't you call Rita and Felton?" I looked at her in surprise. She frowned at me. "Don't look at me like I'm Richard Nixon or something. Do you think I'm totally unfeeling?"

"Should I answer that?"

She slugged my arm, just enough to make it smart, then started making phone calls. Tracy had always excelled in an emergency. For once I was grateful that she was my sister...

* * *

We couldn't find Rita, but Felton was at the ready. He'd been trying to reach me at the office all morning. The Italian loafers we'd stolen from Marilyn's bedroom had mysteriously disappeared. I explained to him about the identities of the skeletons. He didn't seem surprised, but then, nothing much ever surprised Felton.

Charlie decided to go to question Yvonne Cutter about her daughter. Tracy thought she would take Felton and check out Carl's warehouse, but I felt uneasy about this and decided to go with them. I'd left Bree's car at Gourmet Hamburger, so we were stuck with the Bobsled from Hell, but it didn't matter at this point. I put a desperate message to Bree on the answering machine, just in case she should call, but I knew somehow she wouldn't. By the time we located the warehouse the fog had rolled in for the evening, bringing with it the odor of rotting fish that always pervaded the warehouse district. It was November already and within an hour it would be too dark to see much of anything. Felton pulled the car right beneath the rickety fire escape.

"Stinks down here," he commented, wrinkling his nose. I turned to Tracy.

"This probably won't be as much fun as the last time you were here."

She blushed. "Shut up." She tried to get out of the passenger side of the front seat, but not being intimate with the Bobsled from Hell, she had to be coaxed into kicking the door. The handle sprung and she stepped as gracefully as she could into the alleyway.

Felton got out on his side and stared up at the dark building. "Now what?" he asked, looking at me.

I jumped up and snagged the fire escape. "We go in. Look around." Felton glanced doubtfully at Tracy. She was wearing a tight silk skirt and very high heels to show off her legs. She smirked back at him. "I'll wait here," she said.

"Why don't I let you back in the car?" Felton offered politely. Tracy folded her arms and leaned against the grill, ignoring him. Shrugging, Felton followed me up the fire escape to the third floor. The window was still wide open, just as Bree and I had left it almost a month earlier. I slipped through, noticing our scuffmarks against the dust: my long feet, Bree's short ones.

Felton climbed in behind me, scrutinizing the canvassed piles. Nothing seemed to have changed. "Hey, look--" he said, pointing to the floor, "--someone left a flashlight here!"

A shaft of light from my lost flashlight skidded across the dust. "I don't believe it..." I muttered. I got down on my belly and tried futilely to retrieve the traitorous thing, but I still couldn't reach it.

Felton laughed. "Forget it, Rick, I've got one in my car."

I lay there, frozen.

Felton walked over to me. "Rick?"

"Do you smell something?"

"Yeah! It stinks like week-old fish!"

"No!" I pressed my nose closer to the dusty floor. An acrid odor came through the cracks between the planks of wood. "That! Can't you smell it?"

Felton got down on his hands and knees, squeezing down against my face. "Yeah...kinda like sulfur..."

A thin curl of smoke floated up between us. Felton's eyes widened. "Oh my God..."

A high shriek sounded from the floor below us. "HEEELP! HEEEELP!" We jumped up simultaneously and raced to the fire escape. Smoke was pouring from the second-story window. Already Tracy had thrown off her high heels and was scaling the fire escape toward the screams. The three of us reached the window at the same time. I wrapped my coat around my arm and pounded on the glass until it fell out, almost intact.

"*HELP US*!!" The smoke was thick, but I could make out two bound forms lying on the floor. Felton grabbed one and I grabbed the other and we shoved them out of the window at Tracy, who managed to break their falls. Then we carried them down the steps and stuck them into the back seat of Felton's car. The same instinct seemed to drive us all, for Felton promptly twisted the key and we jetted away from the warehouse just as it exploded, sending Perry Sinker's worldly possessions up in flames.

Felton braked the car about four blocks away and we watched, silent, awe-struck, as blue roiling smoke billowed into a vast black cloud above the bay.

From the back seat came a familiar pre-adolescent voice. "*'Bout time you showed up, asshole!*"

I looked back over the torn upholstery to the two figures sprawled on the seat, still bound hand-and-foot. Their faces were smudged with soot, but I recognized their attitude instantly.

"Tracy, Felton. Meet Lonnie and Donnie Zapata."

CHAPTER THIRTY

"You've got a sexy wife, asshole," Lonnie remarked to me, wolfing down his third Big Mac in a row. I'd wanted to take the twins to the local emergency room, but Tracy would have none of it. Instead, she ordered Felton to drive us to my office in the Gas Lamp, then sent him out to *MacDonald's* for some chow. Apparently my mother had told her once that the way to an adolescent boy's heart was through his stomach. So far the twins had finished off six hamburgers and eleven orders of fries. I'd called their mother's house and left word that I'd found them; I expected Delores to come flying through the door at any moment.

"Stick to the subject, Lonnie," Tracy snapped, not being one to suffer fools gladly. "Or I'll take you down to the police station before you finish that burger."

"Hey, we never did *nuthin*'!" Donnie jumped in defensively. "It ain't *our* fault we was there when she bonked him!"

"Yeah!" interjected Lonnie. "We got rights!"

"You've got the right to remain in the cellar of the jailhouse till your feet rot off--" answered Tracy mildly, "--if you don't tell me what I want to know."

"Jeez, lady, you don't have to be so *cranky*..." Lonnie pouted. "I told you already. They was having a fight, just like always, and she pushed him and he pushed her back and then she hit him in the head with that perfume bottle."

"A perfume bottle?" I said incredulously.

"A great big glass one. I think it was Chanel No.5," said Lonnie, obviously relishing the memory. "It didn't even *break*."

"So you're saying that you saw Marilyn Cutter kill Carl Bakersfield?" Tracy asked him impatiently, snatching a French fry from his fingers.

"We didn't know he was Carl. Everyone thought he was Perry."

"And then what happened?"

Donnie jumped in. "Then the big guy, the one we thought was Carl, caught us in the closet watching. Blondie, *she* says they should kill us, but the husband says they should wait and see what happens. I think he was kinda scared that he might need a witness to prove he didn't do the killing." Donnie smiled at his own cleverness and Lonnie patted him on the back proudly. But Tracy wasn't satisfied.

"Whose idea was it to burn the flesh off Carl's skeleton with acid?"

The boys looked at each other uneasily. Tracy smirked. "Oh yes, the chemistry set!"

"They *made* us do it!" shouted Lonnie.

"They *forced* us," Donnie chimed in.

I looked at the two of them, barely thirteen, ragged and streetwise as Notorious Big. In a few years I knew they'd show up on *America's Most Wanted*, but for now Tracy didn't have a legal leg to stand on. Maybe I could talk Delores into taking them back to Texas. I doubted that Texans were quite as lenient as we were here in California when it came to juvenile crime.

I turned to Tracy. "Did you get hold of Charlie?"

She nodded. "He'll be here in a few minutes. He didn't get much out of Mrs. Cutter. She thinks maybe Marilyn intends to take her yacht and skip town. Last she knew, it was anchored down at the Coronado Yacht Club."

The door opened behind us and Rita walked in. When she saw me, Felton, and Tracy hovering over two unwashed, smirking boys, her usual cool countenance shifted a hundred-and-eighty degrees.

"*What the hell?!*"

Lonnie let out a long, admiring whistle. "Babe alert!" Donnie growled lewdly. Rita regained her composure and gave them a look that could freeze mercury.

"Where's Bree?" she asked me pointedly. "I thought she'd be back by now."

I grabbed her arm. "My God! Do you know where she went?"

She extricated herself from my grasp and sat down behind her desk, reaching into her top drawer for a mirror. "She went to have lunch with Marilyn Cutter. I told her Wanda could babysit for her and that I'd be by to pick Wanda up later, but apparently Bree isn't back yet." She checked her make-up, wiped away a smudge, and appeared satisfied. She looked up and saw my face and frowned.

"What's the matter with you, Rick?"

I turned to Tracy. "You explain it to her. I'm going to Coronado!"

Felton, who'd just finishing off Lonnie's French fries, spoke up. "I'll take you."

We started down the stairs. Tracy ran after us. "Don't you want to wait for Charlie?" she shouted.

"Tell him we'll meet him there! And bring help!"

* * *

From the bridge, Felton and I could see the smoke from the warehouse fire, flattened by the incoming fog into an ominous shroud. The Coronado Bridge, one of the longest in the world, arcs from downtown San Diego to a spit of land occupied by millionaires and servicemen known as Coronado Island. It's not a true island, but a peninsula connected to the mainland, attached to Mexico by a narrow sliver of sand known as the Silver Strand.

I'd grown up on Coronado Island, and as far as I was concerned, it was the most beautiful place on earth. Even as a kid I knew I was lucky: walking home from grade school under its splendid palms, riding my bike to its wide white beaches to hunt for crabs, tripping over to the Village Theatre on Saturday night to see the latest Roger Corman horror classic starring Vincent Price. It was the ideal small town then, the classic Ray

Bradbury boyhood set on an island paradise. Then the developers came, and the land speculators, newly-affluent from the Southern California real estate boom of the eighties, and the simple mix of rich and poor became a mix of rich and richer. Bree and I had talked of moving back to Coronado, but my feelings for it were nostalgic, not realistic. Now it was just another fantasy resort.

The Coronado Yacht Club was set across from another famous landmark, the Del Coronado, a luxury hotel built at the turn of the century that had been the site of many a Hollywood film, including "*Some Like It Hot*". My father had actually been on hand for that one, and all he remembered was that everyone on the beach had stared with fascination at a plump blonde woman that he thought had looked rather pale and sickly and unhappy. My Dad had docked a skiff at the yacht club later on, but after I'd emptied the contents on my lunch on his newly-waxed deck the first time he'd shown it to me, he'd decided I probably wasn't the nautical type.

Still, when we reached the Yacht Club, the doorman, Harry, remembered me. He was easily eighty by now, but his teeth were his own and he let me see all of them as he pumped my hand.

"Kinda late to go sailing, ain't it, Ricky?" he grinned, pushing back the gold trimmed uniform cap from his bald forehead. "Too dark to navigate, if you ask me."

"Harry, do you know Marilyn Cutter?"

His grin dissolved immediately and he looked like he'd just bitten into something bitter.

"My ma always said if you can't say something nice--"

"Has she been here tonight?"

"Yeah, as a matter of fact. She and a little redheaded gal were down on *The Night Cry* earlier. Too bad about her daddy, wasn't it?" Harry shook his head. "He was always a fine tipper..."

"Are they still here?"

Harry took off his cap and scratched his naked scalp. "Don't rightly know...guess it'd be okay if you had a look-see..."

He unlocked the gate for us and pointed us down the dock. "She's moored at number 27." We started down the ramp. Harry shouted after us. "Hey, Ricky! Tell that lady she should have her hull scraped!" He went back to his station.

Felton looked at me nervously as we approached the boat. "There's something I think you should know, Rick."

I looked at him expectantly. He stared down at his feet sheepishly. "I can't swim."

"I can't either," I answered grimly.

Felton's eyes widened. "You're kidding! But you grew up on an island!"

"I'm afraid of sharks."

"Then watch out. Here comes one now..." He pointed. I turned and spotted *The Night Cry*. She was large and elaborate, an older, walnut-trimmed sailboat that had been immaculately kept. Her deck lights were off, but through the porthole I spotted a glimmer.

"*Bree*?" I called softly. The night was perfectly still. Fog softened the glow of the street lamps and boat lights; in the distance I heard the mournful call of the foghorn. Gingerly I stepped aboard. I looked back at Felton.

"Stay on the dock if you want."

"I'm coming with you," he said firmly. We walked along the deck until we came to the cabin door. I listened for a moment.

Inside someone sneezed.

Felton and I looked at each other simultaneously, then shoved against the door. It gave easily, throwing us both off-balance, and we went crashing into the cabin. A small kerosene lamp burned on a set of built-in shelves in the corner. Felton and I looked down and saw the source of the sneeze.

It was Ferdinand, the dachshund from hell.

Felton rolled his eyes and stretched out his already-splinted hand, resigned. "Go ahead," he told the mutt, "do your worst."

The little dog looked up at him and whined. Clearly he was cowed by something. He didn't even bother to bare his teeth. Felton frowned. "What the matter with *him*?"

"I don't know." I looked around the cabin, knowing Bree wasn't there. The smell of Marilyn's perfume lingered, though. A flash of white caught my eye. Anchored under the kerosene lamp was a piece of creamy stationery. I recognized Bree's small neat handwriting. Felton peered over my shoulder as I read:

Richard--there's a bomb on this boat. Get off now!

And then we smelled it, mixed with Chanel No. 5: the familiar acrid odor of sulfur. Ferdinand whimpered with fear and I just had time to toss him out the porthole and make a dive off the deck before the yacht exploded. My jacket ignited as I was thrown outward into the bay, but the flame was extinguished by the saltwater before I got burned. I turned, searching for Felton among the jetsam. The flames from the fire shot into the sky, lighting the dock. I could hear sirens and shouting. Harry came running down the boards as fast as his eighty-year old legs would carry him. "Judas Priest!" I heard him mutter. "Judas Priest!"

"*Felton!*!" I shouted. "Felton, where *are* you?" I grabbed an orange lifejacket as it floated past, suddenly realizing that I'd been treading water, a feat I'd never managed to master in swimming class. I squinted out over the black water. "*Felton!*" Behind me I heard a little splashing sound. I jerked around just as Ferdinand dog-paddled past my nose, and following immediately behind him was Felton, grinning and coughing, his hands imitating Ferdinand's paws.

"See, Rick? Nothing to it!"

Within minutes the dock was lined with police cars, their lights flashing. The yacht burned for a few more moments, then sank abruptly. We were fished out of the water by a very confused Coast Guard officer. He put in a call to Headquarters from his boat, then came back to us.

"Are you Richard Matthews?"

I nodded.

He looked at me solemnly. "I've got some bad news for you, sir..."

CHAPTER THIRTY-ONE

Charlie was waiting for me and Felton at the crest of the bridge. Both ends had been blocked off by police cars; it looked as if the entire San Diego force were situated on that narrow span. The coast guard officer escorted me to Charlie's position in the middle lane. I was still soaked from my dip in the bay, and my jacket was scorched. Someone had given me Felton a pink fleecy blanket covered with lambs, and he had it wrapped, medicine-man style, around his shoulders. We were both shivering.

All around us the SWAT team squatted, guns drawn. Several huge spotlights were aimed at the railing, where a tall figure stood, dressed in pants and a shirt and wearing expensive Italian loafers.

Felton gasped. "That's Perry Sinker! That's just the way he looked before he jumped off the bridge, Rick, I swear to God!"

The figure turned toward us and we saw its face now, the savage, beautiful face, ivory hair slicked back, eyes opaque.

"Marilyn..." Felton whispered. "It was *Marilyn all along...*"

Marilyn's right hand was hidden behind the rail, but she didn't appear to be armed. I couldn't understand why the cops didn't rush her. And where was Bree?

Charlie drew me to him. "I don't want you to make any sudden moves..."

"Charlie, what the hell's going on here?"

"Marilyn isn't expecting you, she thinks you're dead. It's a stand-off right now, but she can't hold on forever."

I grabbed his lapels. "What are you talking about?"

Charlie looked at me, his face a mask of tragedy. "She's holding something over the edge of the bridge..."

"What is it? What could be so important?"

"Richard..." His voice cracked. "It's *Bree*..."

I felt my head reeling; it was everything I could do to remain standing. And now I could see that Marilyn stood a little too close to the railing, her hand gripping something that hung suspended a thousand feet over the water, something soft and warm and essential to my life. "Bree!" I cried out before I could help myself.

Marilyn's head snapped up and her eyes narrowed. With the lights facing her she couldn't see me, but clearly she recognized my voice.

"Rick! Slippery Rick! We meet again. Come over closer and say goodbye to your little wifey..."

I looked over to Charlie. He nodded, indicating to his men to hold back. I came forward slowly until I could smell that rich-girl perfume. Marilyn smiled at me slowly, sadistically.

"I should have shot you while I had the chance," she purred. "You've caused me nothing but trouble."

I inched closer to the rail until I could see over it. Bree's white face strained back at me. She dangled as helplessly as a fish on a hook.

"You're right, Marilyn, I've been a pain in the ass, but why take it out on Bree? She's never done anything to you. Let her go."

"That was a poor choice of words, Rick," Marilyn replied. "Perhaps you'd like to rephrase that."

Perspiration began rolling down my side but I kept my voice cool. "You did your best, Marilyn. It just didn't work out. Maybe if Perry had been as smart as you are--"

"Perry was an *idiot*. The only thing Perry knew was explosives. He lacked organizational skills. If it weren't for me, he'd be sitting in a cell somewhere."

"Instead of lying in the morgue?"

Marilyn shrugged. "He got cold feet. He was afraid he'd face a murder charge."

"For killing Razor Moore? And shooting at me?"

Marilyn's smile was genuinely pleased. "Did you think Perry did that? Perry was a big talker, but he didn't have the wherewithal to do what was necessary. Luckily I did..."

"What about Carl? The *real* Carl? Did he do what was necessary?"

Her eye flashed. "He did what I *told* him to! He and Perry were babes in the woods until I came along. Carl wanted his parents out of the way--I arranged it! He wanted a new life, I gave it to him! He should have been satisfied, but he wanted more than I was willing to give him."

"And what was that?"

Her face went rigid. "Me. He wanted *me*..." She looked down at Bree and addressed her in a chiding tone. "You were naughty, weren't you? I dictated that note to you and you *deliberately* ignored me. How did you know that I couldn't read it?"

Bree's voice was thin and far away. "Your mother told me..."

Marilyn's eyes teared up. "A girl can't even trust her own mother..."

I stepped a little closer. "Marilyn, it's over. You can't win now."

She sneered at me. "No, I can't win. But I can make you suffer! You make me *sick* with your sloppy love! Let's see how well you live without it!"

"They'll hang you!"

She shook her head. "Not in this state. Besides, I don't intend to stick around to find out."

She swung her leg over the rail. "Goodbye, Rick. I wish you all the misery your little heart can hold!" With that she silently launched herself off the railing and into the fog.

For a moment there was a stunned silence; then the bridge erupted in a cacophony of sound as SWAT men rushed the railing. Felton crashed into me from behind, his face blank with shock. I couldn't move. My heart had collapsed inside my chest and I felt that surely there was no way it would ever beat again.

I could hear Bree's voice in my mind, its soft timbre vibrating forever through my life, unceasingly, calling my name over and over again. "*Richard... Richard...*"

Felton nudged me and I heard it again, this time not so softly. "*Richard! Pull me up from here!*"

A dozen arms reached over the side of the bridge. Bree chose mine and I hauled her up over the edge of the rail, clinging to her as if my breath depended on it. She was very pale but her heartbeat was steady.

"She had me perched on the ledge," Bree whispered to me. "She never intended to drop me. It was her final joke..."

Charlie instructed his crew to shine the spotlights on the water, but the fog obstructed any real view. Again Marilyn had outwitted us. I wrapped Bree in my arms and walked away. It would be a long time before I'd cross this bridge again...

CHAPTER THIRTY-TWO

Thanksgiving was at our house. I was feeling generous, since Charlie had recently informed me that Carl Bakersfield's aunt was happy to turn the reward money for information about the arson that killed her sister over to *Matthews and Matthews*. Charlie was there with my sister Tracy, and Felton and Rita showed up, although not together. Felton had adopted Ferdinand and wanted to bring him along, but I thought one obnoxious dachshund at the gathering was enough.

Wanda had become our permanent babysitter, a job she was well-suited for, and she helped Bree prepare the turkey. Bree had wanted to invite the Zapata family, but I assured her that they were going home to Texas for the holidays, where I sincerely hoped they would stay. My mother and father showed up for the dinner, but left before dessert, obviously with something more delicious in mind.

Bree's parents apparently liked the Lawrence Welk Retirement Village enough to make an offer on a condominium right next to the golf course. We took them to the airport the day after Thanksgiving, and they assured us they'd be back by Christmas.

At the airport, before their flight arrived, Helen held Margaret in her lap, crooning to her in a low voice as Margaret watched her face breathlessly. I moved in a little closer.

"--and then your Granddaddy took me to the hospital and I told him: I need some music if I'm going to have this baby today, yes sir!"

Margaret giggled with delight.

"--and so he turned on the radio and this darling little girl was singing this darling song. And after the song was over the announcer said: that was *One Step at a Time* by little Brenda Lee! And I said to your granddaddy, if this baby's a little girl, I'm going to name her Brendalee! And sure enough, it was!"

Margaret giggled again.

"And *that's* why I named your mommy Brendalee!"

Margaret clapped her hands together, and hugged Helen fiercely around the neck. "I love you, Grandma!"

"I love you, too, Precious!"

I saw tears come into Bree's eyes. Their flight was announced. Helen and Hugo boarded, weighted down by Waffles in his flight cage and an array of souvenirs. We all cried.

"Don't worry," I told Bree. I hadn't seen her cry in years, and it bothered me. "They'll be back in a few weeks."

"I know," she sniffed, her voice muffled. We got into her Mustang and drove home. My car was still in the shop, recovering from its gunshot wounds. Charlie had located it, finally, at a dump near the Civic Center.

Margaret fell asleep in Bree's lap on the way home. I put her in her crib, tucking her covers close, amazed at how much she'd grown in the past few months. Bree disappeared for a few minutes, then came back into Margaret's room. She handed me a little white plastic cube.

"What's this," I said, puzzled.

"Remember that night Lonnie called? And afterwards?"

I smiled, warming at the memory. "Yeah. I remember. So?"

"*Look* at it, Richard."

I looked. There was a little pink circle in the middle of the plastic cube. A pink circle.

I began to put it together. *Bree's nausea. Her moodiness. That roundness in her face--*

"What does this mean?"

She smiled at me wryly.

"It means," she said deliberately, "--that we're going to have to buy a bigger house."

So we did. But that's another story...

THE END